1

Mr. Lincoln Needs A General

A Novel of the American Civil War

Book Two in the *Lincoln's Generals* Trilogy

by

Michal Howden

Fiction By Michal Howden

The *Lincoln's Generals* Trilogy:

The Wrong Man

Mr. Lincoln Needs A General

In addition:
The Mystery of the Lost Coin

www.michalhowden.com

for my family

all my family

with a special light on my wonderful
wife

without whom not one word would have
been written - MH

Thanks…

I would like to express my sincere thanks to Ms.
Elizabeth Howden and Ms. Dawn Haas Knight for
their unwavering support. I could not (and would not)
have written this without your guidance.
Sincere thanks also go to the lover of the Oxford
Comma, Ms. Jayne Shubat. Thanks for the
outstanding editing and support-again! Above and
beyond, Jayne. Thank you.
A thank you as well to Mr. Topher Howden. Cannot
thank you enough for the design work and helping to
cross the finish line.

Without y'all, the book does not exist. Go Hoosiers.

Covers designed by Mr. Topher Howden

Cover photography by Michal Howden

Chapter 1

"Wait a minute, you lyin' snake-scum!" The rather filthy youngster angrily jabbed a finger at the boy perched above him. "You say you work WHERE?"

The older boy's smug smile grew even larger. Jacob Bunten, late of Salem, Indiana, via The Battle of Bull Run, was lounging on a hogshead outside Willard's Hotel, Washington, D.C. He looked down at his younger companion. "As I said…" he started and then he proceeded to sing at the boy, "Sixteen Hundreeeed Pennsee-VAINIA Avenue…".

The younger boy took a strong step toward the hogshead. Though a bit younger he was not much smaller than Jacob. "Why I oughta…" he threatened, bunching his fists. "You're a bald-faced liar! You not only don't work there; they wouldn't even let you near the place! You couldn't get on the lawn of 1600!"

Jacob airily waved his hand as he gave a small theatrical laugh. "Well," he said to the dirty boy, "after I finish cleaning the street with you, I just may drag you there myself just so you can see, ya little urchin- ya little squirmer!"

The younger boy's fists were instantly raised, "Yeah?" he sneered, "I'd like to see you try! Just try and then we'll see who gets dragged where!"

Jacob dropped off the hogshead, fists at the ready.

The younger boy took an inadvertent step back but then recovered to regain his ground.

Before the inevitable fisticuffs could commence, a man stepped out of Willard's. He was clutching a sheaf of papers. "Jacob!...Jacob!...where are you?" Hearing no immediate response, Thomas Henderson pitched his voice a tone higher. "Stop mucking about! It's time to get back to work."

Hearing those words, Jacob dropped his fists and straightened up. "Yes, sir, Mister Henderson. Yes, sir!" With a sickeningly-sweet, satisfied smile, he looked at his younger adversary, "Are we heading back to the White House to work?"

Thomas gave him a confused look. "Yes." he answered. "Where else would we be heading?" Without waiting for an answer, he turned, tucked his papers under his arm, and began striding up the 1400 block of Pennsylvania Avenue.

Jacob jumped to catch up with his boss. "Yes sir, Mister Henderson!' he called over his shoulder. "Back to the White House it is!" A full smile now filled his face, but his potential adversary didn't see it. Jacob didn't give him so much as a backward glance. Jacob was already sure he'd made his point.

Jacob Bunten may have been pleased that morning, but back at the White House, his employer, President Abraham Lincoln was anything but.

Earlier that morning the president walked into one of his secretaries rooms and mournfully announced, "Well, John, we are whipped again, I am afraid." John Hay looked up from his work. The president gave him a mournful look and continued. "Last night I went to bed, hoping General John Pope had won a great victory. Certainly, he gave us every reason to believe the Army of the Potomac had triumphed." As he spoke his shoulders seemed to shrink inward. "Victory seemed within our grasp," he said in a very sad tone. Then gathering himself, Mr. Lincoln straightened and pulled a telegraph from his pocket. "Here are Pope's words. He said 'We have fought a terrific battle here yesterday. The enemy was driven from the field, which we now occupy.'" The president looked at his secretary before pulling out a second crumpled telegram. He read, "The news just reaches me from the front that the enemy is retreating toward the mountains." Lincoln pulled a third equally crumpled telegram from the pocket. "Ewell is dead and Jackson is badly wounded…"

Lincoln sadly shook his head. "But now it turns out, Ewell is not dead; Jackson is not badly wounded and in fact, Pope, not Jackson is in full retreat. In fact he's retreating from General Jackson as we speak. Now he wires asking, 'I should like to know whether you feel secure about Washington should the army be destroyed.' Should the army be destroyed?! Oh, John,… oh, John, what shall I do? What shall we do?" Mr. Lincoln's agony was apparent, but John Hay could offer no comfort. He had no answers. He could offer no relief.

John Hay shared Mr. Lincoln's despair. John knew that the war was going badly for the North. They had lost the First Battle of Bull Run and Ball's Bluff. They had lost the Peninsula Campaign and now they had lost another battle at Bull Run. True, there had been some successes: Fort Henry, Fort Donelson and Shiloh came to mind, but today those battles seemed like very distant, washed out memories. In July, the army had been at Richmond's gates, over 100,000 strong. Union soldiers, and commanders could hear the city's church bells, for goodness sakes! Now John Hay worried that the only Yankees in Virginia were General Lee's prisoners. A single question haunted him. What in the world had gone wrong?

John Hay was not the only one asking that question during the last days of August, 1862.

Bewildered residents asked each other, "What has happened? What has happened to our army?" Some poised a different question. Some wanted to know, "Who is to blame?"

The soldiers of the army were sure of one thing, this defeat was not their fault. They were certainly not to blame for this fiasco! Thomas and Jacob heard that sentiment loudly, clearly, and directly from the soldiers themselves.

To get first hand information, they decided to seek out an old friend. They had shared previous adventures with Sergeant Emerson of the Second Rhode Island. All three had been at First Bull Run and the Peninsula Campaign. In a manner of speaking, Sergeant Emerson was the reason Thomas and Jacob worked together. The two decided a chat with the good sergeant was in order.

A bit of research let them know the Second Rhode Island was currently posted to Alexandria, Virginia. So they left the White House and headed south along the Potomac River.

Once there, Thomas and Jacob learned that Sergeant Emerson and the Second Rhode Island had not been in the battle. "Now we weren't in the battle, not exactly," Sergeant Emerson confirmed, "but I've heard plenty from them that was. And they tell me we didn't run!" He held up a hand, silencing the two before either could say a word, "Now I know what you're a gonna say, and yes we ran at First Bull Run. A year ago we skeedadled from that battlefield as quickly as rabbits runnin' from a hound! I was scramblin' up the side of that crik and runnin' like a whole lot of other folks. But that was a year ago and we just flat weren't ready then! We were too green and too raw."

Then the sergeant dropped his hand and gave them both a hard look, "And you know as well as anyone, since then we've trained. We've worked hard and we've turned our selves into soldiers. The soldiers at Second Bull Run did not bolt. I've talked to boys from Reno's division, Gibbon's and Kearny's. They all say they retreated in good order."

The good sergeant waited a moment to let those words sink in. "But what they want to know, my dear Mr. Henderson, and this is a good question for you considerin' you now walk with the high and mighty, is why they was put in a place that needed retreatin' from in the first place. Way I hear it, we had at least the same amount of folks, if not more, than the Rebs! It sure looks to us that General Pope got played the fool and outgeneraled. Lee and Jackson made a mockery of him." He shook his head sadly, "A dirty business, Thomas, a dirty business indeed!"

It turned out that many people, civilians and military personnel, both agreed with Sergeant Emerson's conclusion. All around Washington, people were asking, "How did John Pope get put in charge anyway?"

That was a question that John Hay could answer. John knew that after the Peninsula Campaign, Mr. Lincoln had made a decision. After reviewing the five-month campaign, he had decided that the Army of the Potomac needed a new commander. General McClellan was not getting the job done. President Lincoln had decided that General McClellan was not a fighting general. *"He may be a great organizer,"* the president told himself, *"but I need a fighter!"* So a new commander for the Army of Potomac was needed. General McClellan was given lesser duties and President Lincoln's gaze landed on General John Pope. General Pope was from the West, where he had had success opening up sections of the Mississippi River. Partially because of Pope's actions,

Union boats could float as far south as Memphis. That impressed the president. He decided Pope was the man to take command. The president had high hopes for General Pope.

Pope was not well-known in the east, not a member of the Army of the Potomac. The army was not familiar with his ways, he did not understand its culture. His words and actions quickly rubbed many the wrong way.

Pope had little respect for the prior efforts of the army. He made clear that in the west, his soldiers were in action, not training in camps. He let them know he was constantly in motion. He even sent out a pronouncement to that effect. "Headquarters in the saddle," he proudly announced. Many of the soldiers took that phrase in an entirely different way. "Brains in the saddle?" some wagged. "Or some such," agreed another smart-aleck.

Pope also sent these words to the Army of the Potomac. "Let us understand each other. I have come to you from the West, where we have always seen the backs of our enemies." Veterans assumed Pope was referring to the retreats the Army of the Potomac had made during the Peninsula Campaign. "Boys," they muttered to themselves, "those are fighting words!"

Mr. Lincoln said he could put up with the bravado if Pope could deliver victories. He was given command and given directions to defeat the Rebels. Pope immediately went to work preparing plans to defeat Robert E. Lee and the Confederate Army. It was clear to the general that President Lincoln strongly encouraged action. Pope created a plan that was designed to pull Rebel troops away from McClellan, freeing him to make an attack on Richmond.

But as General Lee examined Pope's actions, he made a decision. Based on McClellan's past actions, Lee did not believe McClellan would take advantage of that opportunity. He did not believe the general would move on Richmond. He did not believe the general would move at all. That freed him to turn his back on McClellan and devote his full attention to General Pope.

The result was the battle that became known as the Second Battle of Bull Run. That was the battle Mr. Lincoln was referring to when he told John Hay, "Well, John, we are whipped again, I am afraid." Like other Union commanders, the day started with General John Pope in high spirits. When it ended; however, another Union commander had been defeated by the Rebels and the North had to face another loss.

Many people, like Sergeant Emerson, blamed Pope for the defeat. Other people; however, placed blame in another direction.

Back in the capital a small group of very influential men were discussing generals and the current state of the war. Secretary of War Edwin Stanton, Senator Wade of Ohio, and Senator Chandler of Michigan sat around a table in Stanton's office. None of these men had been McClellan supporters before the battle. They had even more reason to be opposed to the general now.

Stanton was trembling with rage. He pulled a telegram off the table as he rose to his feet. He angrily shook the document at his companions. "Have you read this?" he demanded as he stormed around the room. "It's infamous, it's abhorrent..."

"It's treason, clear and simple," Senator Wade replied. "He should be courtmartialed!"

"He should be shot!" Senator Chandler added.

Stanton took in an asthmatic breath. "General McClellan wrote the president and said we could," and he began to read aloud, "'leave Pope to get out of his scrape! Leave Pope to get out of his scrape!'" he read again, as if he could still not believe it. "Then

McClellan had the audacity to write this message."
Stanton read from a second piece of paper. "'Pope will
be badly thrashed within two days, very badly
whipped he will be and ought to be! Such a villain as
he ought to bring defeat on any cause that employs
him. Once they suffer a terrible defeat and Pope is
disposed of, I know that with God's help, I can save
them.'"

In a low threatening voice, Senator Wade
asked, "Are you quite certain those words came from
General McClellan?" His words were filled with
warning.

"100%!" Stanton affirmed.

"Let me get this straight," Senator Chandler
said. "One general of the Northern Army wants
another general of the Northern Army defeated?

"Not only defeated, Senator, he wants him
badly whipped!"

Chandler shook his head in disgust.

"And gentleman," asked the Secretary, "did
you notice the general's use of pronouns?"

"Pronouns?"

"Yes indeed. Listen again! 'Once *they* suffer a
terrible defeat and Pope is disposed of, I know that
with God's help I can save *them*.'"

"Ah." said Chandler.

"They and them instead of saying us and ours." said Wade.

Stanton asked, "Does the man not realize we're all on the same side? Does the man actually want us to lose?"

"There you may have hit it, Edwin," Senator Chandler said. "I've come to realize that McClellan only believes in McClellan and to hell with everyone else!"

"And no," Senator Wade chipped in, "I do not believe that McClellan does believe in the same war we're fighting." He rose from his chair and faced the men. "You know about his Harrison's Landing letter. You know he told the president we should go easy on the South. You know he wants to let the South return. He wants to reconstruct the Old Union, just as it was."

"And he means to preserve slavery!" said Chandler, a rabid abolitionist.

"Restore the Old Union?" Stanton nearly shouted. "After a year of war? Are you mad? Is he mad? He wants us to just let those states that declared rebellion, those states that left the Union, those states that killed our soldiers, just wander back in without so much as a la-di-da?" He glared at his two companions. "Over my dead body!"

"It's scandalous!" agreed Chandler.

Though not quite as vehement as Misters Stanton, Chandler, and Wade, John Hay also believed that McClellan would not do. Clearly, new leadership of the Army of the Potomac was demanded. But the key question, the one that had vexed the president the entire war was, who? Who was the right man to lead the fight?

John Hay decided it was time to help the president answer that question. John thought it was time to do a little work, get a little research done.

John left his office and walked down the hall. He tapped at a door frame, interrupting the two occupants. "Thomas, Jacob, good morning," Hay said, "Sorry to interrupt, but Thomas I have a task for you if you're willing and have the time."

Thomas stood up. "Of course sir, anything you need."

John took a step into the room motioning Thomas to take his seat. "Now Thomas, we've talked about this. I'm not a Sir, I'm just John Hay from Salem, Indiana." He gave Jacob a smile. Jacob still considered it an almost unbelievable coincidence that he and John Hay happened to be from the same Indiana town. Hay turned back to Thomas, "So it's John, please."

Thomas nodded his understanding. "How can I help, John?"

"Well, Thomas, it's just a small thing. I need you to find the Tycoon a general to lead his army, that's all."

Jacob reacted before Thomas could. "What!?"

John laughed. "All right, calling it a small thing may be a bit of an overstatement. Here's what I need. Can you compile a list of men who should be considered as a possible commanding general of the Army of the Potomac? It would be a list we could consult if we ever found ourselves needing such a thing. Can you do that?"

Thomas was a good researcher and a good writer. He had proven that before. And this was an assignment that he was sure needed to be done. "Yes sir,…I mean yes, John, I can certainly do that."

"And I can help!" Jacob asserted.

"So be it. I look forward to reading it." He turned to leave but stopped short, turning back to them. "And I don't think we need to bother the president with this quite yet, do you?"

"Oh, no sir, no need at all."

"Good, good, let me know when you have something to share."

Chapter 2

The next day, Thomas presented John Hay with a list of names. Hay was impressed with Thomas' speed. He quickly read the document. "What's the order, I mean how do you have them ranked?"

Thomas gave John a surprised look. "Oh no, sir, I wouldn't presume…"

John Hay interrupted him. "First of all, it's John, not sir" and he gave Thomas a bit of a look "and secondly, of course you should rank them. I need your input and reasoning."

With an embarrassed smile, Thomas handed John another sheet of paper.

"Ah, yes, much better. Let's see, Halleck, Kearny, Reynolds, Burnsides, Hooker, Fremont ah…" John reached for a pencil and drew a line through Fremont's name, "I'm afraid with his history Fremont won't do. So let's see," he said returning to the list, "Porter, Reno…" Hay looked up. "Very nice job, Thomas, very nice. But I notice all the generals are from the East. No candidates from the West? I mean I know Pope did not work out but…?"

"Well, John, there was one name that I thought about, General U.S. Grant. Fort Henry, Donelson, and

Shiloh, after all, but when I did a bit of research and read official reports it seemed that the credit for those victories belonged to General Halleck."

"Hmmph. Well, as you say then," said Hay.

Jacob had been sitting quietly, listening to the discussion. He appeared to be very puzzled. He jumped in, "Hey, how do we get generals anyway?"

The question startled Thomas. He gave an involuntary shake of his head, a horse shaking off a fly. John Hay laughed.

Thomas answered first. "They come from West Point and from the army. You know, prior military service."

John nodded his head in agreement, "They do indeed. They also come from other places. In this war you see, we have different types of generals."

"Different types?" Jacob asked. "I thought a general was a general."

"Oh most assuredly not!" John answered. "We have a couple of different types in our army. Some of our generals are military generals, military experts. Just as Thomas said, these generally, excuse the bad pun, come from West Point or the army. We have several who started as lieutenants and now have made their way up to general."

"Like General McClellan," Thomas interjected.

"Exactly like our own General McClellan. But we need another type of general as well. I call these generals *'political generals'*. They may not bring any military experience, but they bring other things that are just as valuable."

"Now that makes no sense!" Jacob said.

"Perfectly understandable, Jacob. It's an odd concept. But they are appropriately named because in most cases their appointments go straight back to politics. For instance, you know that President Lincoln won the election of 1860?"

Jacob gave Hay a hard look. "Of course I do!" Jacob said indignantly.

"Of course, of course," Hay said soothingly. "But do you know how many votes he won by?"

Jacob scrunched his face, "You mean the exact number of votes? Now who in the world walks around with that number taking up valuable space in their heads?"

Henderson and Hay both laughed at that.

"Excellent point, Jacob! That would be a waste of valuable brain space. Let me be more clear. Approximately three million votes were cast and Mr. Lincoln won about sixty percent of them."

"So he got the most, fair and square!" Jacob asserted.

"Well it rather depends on how you look at it. It's a question of numbers, you see. We believe that almost seven million people had the right to vote in 1860. If you take that number and realize Mr. Lincoln received about a bit less than two million of those votes, Mr. Lincoln was able to convince only about twenty-two percent of the voters to support him. Flip that coin and you see that seventy-eight percent did not. And I know, as you know, seventy-eight percent is a lot bigger than twenty-two percent. In other words, and if you'll permit me to round off a bit, perhaps 5 million Americans did not vote for Mr. Lincoln while some 2 million did."

"Wait, wait, wait," Jacob said incredulously, "Are you saying Mr. Lincoln lost the election?"

"No, no," Hay quickly responded. "Mr. Lincoln won fair and square as you said, but we have to be aware of those numbers. We can't ignore them. Well, to be truthful we can ignore the Southern voters, none of them voted for Mr. Lincoln. Heck, his name wasn't even on the ballot in several of those states. But if we look at the people who did vote, forty percent did not choose Mr. Lincoln. Now we need that forty percent, or as much of it as we can get, to support the war and Mr. Lincoln's efforts."

Thomas jumped in. "Jacob we've talked about the Democrats in Congress. Think of this, most of them voted for Stephen A. Douglas in the last election. Now we need them to come around, support Mr. Lincoln, the Republicans and the war effort. "

"Exactly right, Thomas. So if we happen to select a democrat, a man popular in Democratic politics I should say, to serve as general in the army, well," Hay made an up and down balancing motion with his hands, "that just might make us a few friends, just might generate a little support. Having a Democrat like General Butler from Massachusetts or General Sickles from New York is an example."

"The Democrats are just one example. There are lots of groups who can help or hurt the war effort," Thomas said.

"Sure are." Hay agreed, "For example, look at the immigrants. Lots of Germans came over here and have now joined the Union Army. Why we even have regiments where they speak German instead of English. If we have a general with German blood or German connections, they appreciate that. That's why we have General Sigel."

"Right!" said Thomas. "We even have to curry favor with Republicans. Look at the radical republicans. A general who supports them will, in turn, draw their support. General Fremont is a good example of that!"

"To be truthful," John Hay said, "we can't do it by ourselves."

Jacob had listened patiently, math and all. But now he gave a disgusted snort. "Well, just fine then!" Jacob said. "If we have military generals and political generals, why is it so all-fired danged hard to find a good one?" He crossed his arms, leaned back in his chair, and waited for an answer.

"From the mouths of babes!" laughed Hay. "Well, Jacob, let's concede military generals usually make the most effective fighting generals. Let's focus on them. Now, most people don't realize that West Point only graduates between forty and sixty cadets a year so the pool to pick from is really not as large as you might think. And then," he continued, "West Point cadets come from all over the country, so as you can well imagine, a lot of those graduates were from the South." He lowered his voice a notch. "A lot of those graduates went south." Hay ticked the ends of his fingers as he counted off, "Lee, who not only graduated West Point, but served as its superintendent." He paused to give Jacob a pointed look. "Longstreet, Jackson, Stuart, etc."

Jacob gave Hay a sour look. "Well, they sure seemed to get all the good ones!"

Hay laughed again, "So I've been told, Jacob, so I've been told. Heck, we even have graduates from northern states serving in the Confederate Army. But we have a few West Point graduates ourselves." The fingers were extended again, "McClellan..."

"Ugh!' Jacob interrupted.

"Jacob!" Thomas admonished.

Hay gave Jacob a look that was meant to be severe, but there was a sparkle in his eye.

"Ahem," he said "if I may continue. McClellan, Halleck, Thomas, and Hooker, to name a few. The South didn't get all the good ones."

"Hmm, matter of opinion there!" Jacob muttered, just loudly enough to be heard.

"Jacob!" Thomas admonished again.

Jacob dropped his head. "Sorry, Mr. Henderson." But no one in the room really thought he meant it.

Jacob was not alone in his assessment. It turned out that Secretary of War Stanton agreed with Jacob, though of course they'd never discussed the matter. And Stanton was taking action. He wanted McClellan out, and he decided that Mister Lincoln's Cabinet needed to prod the president in that direction. Stanton knew that the Cabinet would be meeting in a very few days and he wanted to be ready. So Stanton, ever the lawyer, began drawing up a declaration. The paper would declare that McClellan should not, under any circumstances, be given command of the army again. If Stanton had his way, the paper would say McClellan should be dismissed from the army.

Stanton wrote a first draft and proceeded to meet with his fellow cabinet members. After Attorney General Bates made his contribution, it read, "The undersigned do but perform a painful duty in declaring to you our deliberate opinion, that at this time, it is not safe to trust to Major General McClellan the command of any armies of the United States." Four of the six cabinet members present signed. Gideon Welles refused to sign, saying he believed such a statement was disloyal to the president, but agreed that if called upon, he would announce his support for the position.

Stanton quietly thanked the cabinet members. Inside however, he was ecstatic. *"Fine then, fine,"* he thought, *"perhaps, just perhaps, I have the tool I need to get rid of McClellan."*

But he did not. While he was working his magic, the president was also making decisions. And the president had decided he needed McClellan.

As the president evaluated the situation, he found himself, as he put it, between that rock and that hard spot. The president had grave worries about McClellan. He had become furious when he heard McClellan's comments about seeing Pope "badly whipped". But the president was also very aware that a large Rebel army was just a few miles from Washington, D.C. General Pope was worried about his army being destroyed. General Halleck, brought in to run the war, seemed to Lincoln to have lost "his nerve and pluck." The city was in a state of turmoil after the defeat. Rumors flew everywhere.

"Lincoln is running to Philadelphia; Washington is falling."

"100,000 Rebels are marching toward us right now!"

"200,000 Rebels surround us right now!"

"The army is destroyed; the Confederates have won!"

Lincoln had stood on this precipice before. He had come close to dismissing McClellan after the Peninsula Campaign. But it came down to the same issue. Yes, McClellan had acted abominably, but Mr.

Lincoln needed that army and in his opinion, General McClellan was the best man to deliver it. He had come to the painful conclusion that he needed General McClellan. Perhaps it was more accurate to say the Army of the Potomac needed him, but upon consideration, he decided, weren't those both one in the same?

Now the president knew that if you wanted action, McClellan was not a good choice. He also knew that the general was only interested in his own agenda. *"No,"* Lincoln thought, *"that's not fair. He believes in a different Union than I have come to believe in."* He also knew that McClellan hated to see injury to his army. Nothing wrong with that in theory, but in reality, Mr. Lincoln knew that the army had to be used if it was to win. If they were to defeat the Rebels, Lincoln well knew casualties would be involved.

"No, McClellan would be not the long term answer but I do believe he will be a short-term answer. I do not believe we can end the rebellion with him in charge. But I do believe that we can defend the capital with him in charge and that's what I need tomorrow!"

Chapter 3

September 02, 1862 started like any other work day for Thomas and Jacob. They left their lodgings at the Dodge House and started walking to the White House.

The arrival of September might have meant cooler days in some parts of the Union, but September was hot and humid in the Union's capital. The day threatened rain. The humidity was intense, even in the day's early hours. Thomas and Jacob were soaked in sweat by the time they made their way to 1600.

The two made their way to the room that served as their work station. It was too much to call it an office. It was a small rectangular space tucked under a stairway. A person who stood up too quickly or without paying attention might well earn a bonk as his head met the slanted ceiling. The space was just large enough to hold a table, desk, and two chairs. It was cramped, but still, it was theirs.

Jacob made his way to the table that served as his headquarters in the White House. He dutifully settled in to start working, but he kept one eye on the door. He was waiting for his real work to begin. Jacob was proud of the fact that several people around the

White House, including Mr. Lincoln, called on him to do their bidding out and about in Washington, D.C. Experience had taught him that he wouldn't have long to wait.

Thomas meanwhile went to the shelf, grabbed his glazed tankard, and filled it with water. Then he seated himself at his desk and started to sort through the various telegraphs and reports that had made their way to the White House during the overnight hours.

Thomas read and his hands slid back and forth, organizing the papers. One stack was destined for John Hay, another for John Nicolay, a smaller stack was for the War Department. Those were usually duplicates of dispatches the War Department had already received, but better to be safe than sorry Thomas thought. By far, the largest pile was for the president himself. Mr. Lincoln wanted to see everything.

Suddenly, Thomas jerked back in his chair as if an electric current had surged through his body.

Jacob instantly saw this unusual reaction. Thomas was not moving. He sat frozen in his chair. A piece of paper was clutched in his hands, but it was obvious he was no longer seeing it. And then, to

Jacob's amazement, Thomas began moaning, low, slow sorrowful moans.

Jacob now sat frozen. He had no idea what to do or how to react. He had never seen Thomas like this. Slowly he rose from his creaking chair and took a small step forward. "Mr. Henderson?" he tentatively inquired. "Mr. Henderson, what's wrong?"

Thomas clutched at his chest, trying his best to regain control. Without saying a word he thrust the paper in Jacob's direction.

Jacob read the dispatch, as quickly as possible trying to find the source of his friend's distress. His eyes raced down the page. Then his knees nearly buckled as he saw the words, "General Kearny killed in action near Chantilly, Virginia."

"*No it can't be!*" he instantly thought. "*Kearny can't be dead!*"

General Philip Kearny had befriended both Jacob and Thomas during the Peninsula Campaign. Jacob was sure Kearny had saved Thomas' life by moving him from a field hospital to a commandeered house in Norfolk, Virginia. He had also treated Jacob with great kindness. Kearny was one of the North's heroes. Kearny couldn't be dead!

But the reports proved to be true. Kearny had been killed during the Battle of Chantilly.

The Battle of Chantilly was the last gasp of Second Bull Run. Evidently, during a driving evening rainstorm, Kearny had decided to ride out to reconnoiter.

"But General, the risk!" cried an aide.

Kearny replied, "The Rebel bullet that can kill me has not yet been molded."

Amidst thunder and lightning Kearny rode forward. Soon he rode into troops.

They were Confederate troops.

They ordered him to surrender, but in typical Kearny fashion, he ignored their demand. He whirled his horse about to race back to Union lines. The Confederates opened fire. General Kearny fell from his saddle.

Confederate Major General. A.P. Hill ran to the gunfire. Examining the body, he removed his hat and said to the men, "You've killed Phil Kearny; he deserved a better fate than to die in the mud." When Stonewall Jackson arrived he said, "My God, boys, do you know who you have killed? You have shot the most gallant officer in the United States Army. This is Phil Kearny, who lost his arm in the Mexican War." General Lee himself made sure that Kearny's body was sent back to the Union forces, with a condolence note.

Jacob and Thomas were both despondent. It was true they had lost a man who meant much to them. In addition, they also realized the North had lost a great general. Thomas had previously talked with John Hay about placing General Kearny in a position of greater responsibility. Jacob had chimed in, proclaiming, "Kearny is a fighter!" He didn't say *"and McClellan isn't!"* but he didn't have to. His implication was clear. Jacob most strongly felt that General Kearny should have already replaced General McClellan. Now Kearny was dead.

Thomas immediately blamed McClellan for Kearny's death. It was true Pope was commanding the army but in Thomas' opinion, McClellan had refused to help Pope, thus insuring his defeat. Without that defeat there would be no Battle of Chantilly and Kearny would still be alive. Now Thomas and Jacob were more certain than ever, General McClellan had to go!

But the man who made that decision, President Lincoln, did not know about the Battle of Chantilly or General Kearny's death. Before Thomas and Jacob had even arrived at the White House that morning, the president and General Halleck were on their way to General McClellan. The decision had been made. Mr. Lincoln asked General McClellan to assume command of the Army of the Potomac and the general had agreed to '*save the country*' one more time.

A bit before noon that day, the members of cabinet began assembling. But when the clock stuck noon, the official start time for the meeting, the president was uncharacteristically absent. A few minutes passed before the door opened and President Abraham Lincoln entered the room. "Excuse me gentlemen, sorry to be late." Lincoln walked to a side table and deposited his hat and papers. "I have some news that I am sure some of you will find troubling." Mr. Lincoln took a bit of a breath and turned to fully face the men around the main table. "Gentlemen, General Halleck and I have just returned from a meeting with General McClellan. He has been reinstated and has resumed command of the Army of the Potomac."

There was a stunned silence in the room before Stanton spoke. In a slightly strangled voice, Stanton said, "No order to that effect has been issued from the War Department."

"No, Mister Secretary that order came from me. I've ordered General McClellan to take command. The order is mine and I will be responsible for it to the country."

Then the other men in the room erupted. "McClellan wanted Pope to lose. We can't reward him!"

"Mr. Lincoln! Stanton nearly shouted, "McClellan is incompetent and quite possibly a traitor!"

Secretary Chase chimed in. "I cannot but feel that giving command to McClellan is equivalent to giving Washington to the Rebels."

Mr. Lincoln let them have their say before he responded. "Gentlemen, I hear your comments, and I must say I agree with much of what you say. I most certainly appreciate your earnest sincerity. McClellan's actions concerning the latest battle are very disturbing. He has acted badly in this matter, and I know that. *But* we must use the tools we have. There is no man in the army who can lick these troops of ours into shape half as well as he. Unquestionably, he has acted badly toward Pope. He wanted him to fail. That is unpardonable. But General McClellan is too useful just now to sacrifice. I must have McClellan to reorganize the army and bring it out of chaos."

"But Mister Lincoln!" Stanton interrupted.

"No, Edwin! There is no other choice. Pope had the army only 74 days and nearly destroyed it! The Rebels are within miles of the city! We need a commander now. Today. And gentlemen, McClellan has the army with him." Mister Lincoln paused to look at each cabinet member. And then he repeated, "Gentlemen, I say again, McClellan has the army with him. No, I am sorry but we must use the tools we have. I need McClellan."

And President Lincoln was right. The Cabinet may have been dismayed, but much of the military became exuberant when they heard the news.

To let his troops know that he was back, General McClellan dressed in his best uniform, complete with bright-yellow sash and summoned his aides. They mounted and galloped down the road toward the Army of the Potomac. Of course he was instantly recognized by his men and cries erupted up and down the lines. "Boys, McClellan is back in command. Hip, hip!" Troops cheered, caps were thrown in the air and the malaise of defeat evaporated. Suddenly, all was right with the men of the Army of the Potomac.

But when Thomas and Jacob heard the news, they were plunged even further into depression. They both deeply believed in Mr. Lincoln, but as Thomas said, "Jacob, it's a hard thing to swallow."

The younger man instantly agreed, "A hard thing, indeed."

Chapter 4

"Look, you," John Nicolay said to John Hay. The two sat in Nicolay's office at the White House, watching a late afternoon thunderstorm pelt the windows with rain. "This is a short-term assignment. I heard the Ancient say, 'Well if he can't fight himself, he excels in making others ready to fight.' Mr. Lincoln is merely using General McClellan as a short-term defensive tool. His job is to prevent Lee from attacking this city and after that...well after that, we're done with our Little Napoleon."

"If only I was as sure," Hay replied, "so far this war has had a strange way of turning things upside down."

As they watched events occur over the next few days, it appeared John Nicolay was correct in his assessment. McClellan did indeed begin to once again whip the army into shape. He inspected the Washington, D.C. area forts, he inspected the troops, he ordered his officers to "inspect everything!" The men forgot all about Pope and the defeat at the Second Battle of Bull Run.

And Nicolay was right about the president's assessment of McClellan. Lincoln told them, "He'll not be the aggressor, but I believe he can get the men ready to defend this city. And that is what I am asking him to do."

Across town, Thomas was having lunch with some officers he'd met during the Peninsula Campaign. They were discussing the current situation. They were assuring Thomas that strengthening the city's defenses was the top priority. "Thomas, it might not even come to blows. This city is so entrenched, I don't think Lee would consider attacking."

"Look, it's already September. Both armies are bloodied. Why, I wouldn't be surprised in the least if we started making winter camp any day now. Time enough to fight next spring."

Lt. Colonel Alexander Webb shook his head at that, "I don't know about winter camp, but I do know the spirits of the men are up. I don't mean to criticize Generals Pope or McDowell, but fairly or not, many of the men felt let down by their generals. Now with Little Mac back, they have their confidence renewed."

Thomas had realized long ago that Alexander Webb was a gentleman and a nice person to boot. He was not surprised that he would not criticize Generals Pope or McDowell. But Thomas had heard plenty of criticism from others and he knew that many, like

Sergeant Emerson, believed that they had been 'out-generaled'. Though Thomas still distrusted McClellan, and blamed him for Kearny's death, he had to take a hard swallow and admit once again that McClellan may have been the only choice for the job.

When Thomas returned to work, he found Jacob perched on his chair, chewing on a pencil.

"Lunch not filling?" he asked.

Jacob gave him a puzzled look.

Thomas pointed to the pencil. "I was merely asking if you got enough for lunch since I see you chewing on a pencil."

Jacob seemed a bit distracted. "Uhmm, lunch was tolerable, thanks."

"Okay, Jacob, what gives?" Thomas walked over and stood right next to Jacob, giving him his full attention.

Jacob turned the pencil around a few times. "Well, I guess I have a question." He looked at Thomas who nodded his head. "What does e-man-see-pay-tion mean," he asked, sounding out the word "and what's the difference between a hard war and a soft war?"

That took Thomas aback. "Goodness me, where did these questions come from? Lunch?"

"Kind of, well not exactly. See, Mr. Dana stepped in while I was eating and asked if I could do an errand for him. I told him I'd be glad to, and he told me to drop by his office when I finished. So I went down, but when I got there John and John…"

Thomas pounced as swiftly as a diving hawk. "John and John? Please, please, please do NOT tell me you mean *Mr.* Hay and *Mr.* Nicolay. Please tell me we are talking about two other completely different individuals I don't know!"

Jacob had the decency to look slightly chagrined and duck his head. "Sorry Mr. Henderson, of course I mean Mr. Nicolay and Mr. Hay…anyway I heard them use those words and I didn't know what they meant."

An irritated Thomas pushed on. "You mean you were eavesdropping?"

Jacob's hands flew up in his defense. "No sir, no eavesdropping whatsoever. They asked me to wait in the hall, I knew Mr. Dana wanted me. The door was open…" he dropped his hands and gave a shrug as if asking "What else was I to do?"

Thomas stood his ground, trying to decide what, if any, action was required. He ran through it all again and decided there was really no harm done. The White House had an open door policy to virtually anyone. Thomas was still amazed that almost anyone could open the front door of the White House, walk in and wander around, looking for the president's office. Mr. Dana, Mr. Hay and Mr. Nicolay knew the situation. If they decided to have a conversation next to an open door, well, then where's the damage? And that John and John? He'd long ago come to accept that Jacob was a bit impertinent. It might have reminded him of someone else, if he'd cared to admit it, which he currently did not.

Thomas relaxed a bit. When Jacob saw that, he relaxed a little himself. Thomas said, "Let me finish a bit of work and I will be glad to try and answer your questions." He turned back to his desk, grabbed the paper he had been working on, perused it, and then added a few sentences. He then offered the paper to Jacob. "Now, when we're finished with this discussion, will you please run this to Mr. Nicolay?"

"Yes, sir!" came the instant and energetic reply.

Thomas gave a small grimace and then turned his chair around to fully face Jacob. He lifted a forefinger up. "First, emancipation means to free someone. Hard war versus…"

"Wait," Jacob interrupted. "who we freeing?"

"Jacob, do you want me to continue or not?" Thomas snapped, annoyed at the interruption. But mid-way into his reply, he really heard Jacob's question. He paused. *If indeed, the trio was discussing emancipation, who was being emancipated? The rebel states? The rebel soldiers? Absolutely Not!*

And then the most obvious, yet impossible thought came to him. *Were they discussing freeing the slaves? Impossible! Well, wasn't it?* That thought caused his head to spin. *How, what, when…what were they even talking about?*

Jacob waited as Thomas ran those thoughts around his head. But then, getting no further answer, Jacob tried his second question, "Well then, what about hard and soft war?"

"Uhmm…" a somewhat distracted Thomas started, "yes, well, as I understand it, there are two views, at least two, on how the war should be fought. Some people believe that if we just give the South the chance to reconsider, they will come back into the Union and things can be as they were before Fort Sumter. They say General McClellan believes this, for instance. That's the soft war.

Others believe however that the time for soft war is long gone and we must do everything we can to compel the South to stop their efforts to destroy the Union. Every tool must be used, and people must realize we are not going back to the old Union, back to the old ways..." Thomas stopped in mid-sentence. Suddenly the pieces came together. He suddenly thought he understood how hard and soft war fit with emancipation. *No, it was outlandish! Could he possibly be correct? It didn't seem possible, but then...*He decided he needed confirmation.

"You say Mr. Dana was in his office?"

"Well, he was a few minutes ago," Jacob confirmed.

"Thank you, I have...I need.." and Thomas left their room without another word.

"Now what in the world?" Jacob wondered and returned to gnawing on his pencil.

Thomas made his way down to Mr. Charles Dana's office. He walked with a bit of trepidation. He'd only met the man a short time ago and Mr. Dana had been most welcoming. But still, Thomas had heard the name Charles Anderson Dana all his life. Mr. Dana was an important member of the *New York Tribune*. As a native New Yorker, Thomas was very familiar with his work.

Dana had left the *Tribune* and become a special Investigating Agent of the War Department. In spite of the impressive title, he treated Thomas as an equal. He embarrassed Thomas in fact when he told people that he and Thomas were both New York journalists.

"Far from it!" Thomas would protest. Being a part time contributor to the *New York Constitutionalist* did not compare to the storied career Mr. Dana had built at the *New York Tribune*.

The door was open when Thomas arrived so he knocked on the door frame. Dana looked up from his reading. "Thomas, come in. I was just down in your neck of the woods chatting with Jacob. Come in, come in."

"So I hear, sir. That's actually the reason I hoped I might have a word. Do you have the time?"

Dana swept a small stack of papers from a chair. "Please make yourself comfortable." He waited until Thomas was seated before continuing, "Now, how can I help?"

"Well sir, Jacob asked me a question and I was not sure about the correct answer. It has to do with emancipation."

Dana paused for a minute and then a smile broke across his face. "Did that scalawag overhear us talking?"

"Uhhmmm," Thomas began, hoping to keep Jacob out of trouble.

"No, no, Thomas, the fault is ours. No blame to Jacob at all. We should know better. Still it is no great state secret either so that's that." He leaned back and stroked his beard, "Well, yes, emancipation. It was the topic of our discussion. The president is currently considering the idea."

"What can you tell me sir,.. I mean I understand the meaning of the word, but I'm not sure who or what is being freed?"

Mr. Dana thought for a moment and then leaned toward Thomas. His eyes gleamed with excitement. "The slaves, Thomas. Mr. Lincoln wants to free the slaves. Well, to be precise, not all of them right now, but yes, Mr. Lincoln is thinking about such an action."

Now it was Thomas' turn to lean back and consider.

"How can that be, sir? Mr. Lincoln campaigned on not interfering with slavery and said as much in his inaugural address. He sure made it sound like there was nothing he could do about slavery."

"So he did Thomas. But he also made it clear he would not condone secession and secession has now been attempted. No, we're in different days now Thomas a different world."

Thomas was truly confused. "But what does that mean, Mr. Dana?"

"Ah, there are so many sides to this thorny problem." He thought for a minute and said, "Let me take you back a bit and maybe we can understand where we've ended up today." He took a deep breath and began.

"I truly believe that Mr. Lincoln has been against slavery much of his life. I think he believes it is an ugly, disgusting, abominable practice. But I also know he understands the United States Constitution and understands that that document makes slavery legal in this country. Hence the statement, 'I will not interfere with slavery where it exists.'"

"However, I believe he follows Thomas Jefferson's lead and believes that we can limit the expansion of slavery. Look at the Northwest Ordinance. That document outlawed slavery in the area that became the states of Ohio, Michigan, Indiana, Illinois, and Wisconsin. So Mr. Lincoln believes, as Mr. Jefferson did, that it is legal to limit the growth of slavery. And that's where he stood before his election. Then of course, the southern states changed everything with their rebellion."

Thomas was doing his best to follow. "But what difference does that make? If it was illegal to free the slaves before the war, why is it legal to free them now? The Constitution didn't change."

"Well, it hasn't yet, " Dana said cryptically. "But the South's action changed the situation. You see when they seceded, fired the first shots at Fort Sumter, and started the war, they changed the situation."

Thomas gave him a puzzled look. "Look at it this way," Dana continued. "Let's say a Southern worker, a worker supporting secession, steps away from his plow and orders a slave to pick that plow up and continue the work. Then that southern worker, that Rebel, is free to pick up a rifle, a rifle he uses to shoot at our boys. He gets to become a soldier and the work still gets done. If the slaves aren't doing the work the South depends on, it would weaken their war effort, thereby making it easier to defeat them and reunite the Union."

"But doesn't that change the purpose of the war?" asked Thomas.

"Not at all!" Dana quickly answered, "the purpose of the war was and is to reunite the Union."

"Hmmm," Thomas worried. "Yes, I can see that, but I also can see that a lot of our soldiers won't see it that way! They joined to preserve the Union, not fight over slavery. My worry is that they will think you are asking them to die for the Negro."

"Then it's our job to help them understand! They need to see that every time a slave does an ounce of work, it frees a Reb soldier to pull the trigger of his rifle. We need to remind our soldiers that those rifles are pointed at them!"

"So this really is part of that hard war, soft war debate."

"Oh, there's no more debate on our part, Thomas. We tried the soft war, it did not work. It did not compel the South to lay down their arms. Now we've come to realize it will take a total effort to defeat such a foe and every weapon in our arsenal must be used. We won't go back to the way of life before 1860. It's time to take the nation forward!"

It turned out Thomas and Jacob were not the only ones with questions. Across the country, more and more people were talking about emancipation.

Politicians who opposed the war, North and South, knew Mr. Lincoln was being pressured to free the slaves. They were quick to throw Lincoln's words in his face. In his inaugural address the president had said, "I have no purpose, directly or indirectly to interfere with the institution of slavery in the states where it exists. I believe I have no lawful right to do so, and I have no inclination to do so."

"Nothing has changed!" they scoffed, "Lincoln still had no right to take any action against the slaves."

On the other side of the argument, abolitionists
and Northerners were increasing their pressure on the
president. They wanted him to free all the slaves and
free them right now. They maintained slavery had
caused the rebellion and without slavery, the South
could not continue to rebel. Republican leaders such
as Thaddeus Stevens had been pushing for immediate
emancipation for the last eight months. It was well
known that these men shared their views with Mr.
Lincoln on a regular basis.

And Mr. Lincoln had indeed been thinking
about emancipation. He supported paying slave
holders for their slaves. In fact, in April 1862,
Congress declared that the federal government would
compensate slave owners who freed their slaves.
Slaves in the District of Columbia were freed on April
16, 1862, and their owners were compensated. But
other slave owners were quick to reject this idea of
compensation. Daunted, but not willing to give up,
Mr. Lincoln continued to "noodle on the problem."

In July of 1862, Lincoln met with his Cabinet to
tell them he had been "pondering the issue of
emancipation. Now, my policy is not ready for
review," he told them, "but it's progressing."

At the next Cabinet meeting, the president
announced that he felt compelled to issue a paper on

the subject. The Cabinet was split on the merits of this idea, but they did agree on one thing, the timing. They agreed that if the president issued it now, after such a defeat as Second Bull Run, it might well look the last desperate action of a defeated nation. "Delay the release of any paper until the Union Army wins a victory," they advised. And of course, some Cabinet members went even further, emphatically advising him not to present it at all.

Mr. Lincoln went to work. He crystalized his thinking over the weeks and created a rough draft of a proclamation on emancipation. In it, he offered the south 60 days to put down their arms and rejoin the Union. If they did not, on day 61, all of their slaves would be declared free. When he was comfortable with his work, he presented it to the Cabinet.

The Cabinet members instantly erupted with a cascade of complaints and questions. "Why only free slaves in the South? What about the border states? Why were they excluded? How would this be accomplished? Wasn't it an empty threat since they did not control all of those states? So by definition, wasn't it an empty statement?"

"Excellent points, gentlemen, but let me be clear. I've decided on the policy. I'm only asking for your input into the word smithing! My mind on this matter is firm. But to answer your questions, I'm issuing this proclamation as the Commander in Chief. Therefore, it applies only to those who carry out war against us. That is why the border states are excluded. They do not carry out war against us.

But my experts tell me we have approximately 4 million slaves in this country, and 3.5 million of them live in those rebelling states. So it is a strong first step. And yes, it is true that we do not control all of that land today. But that will change and when it does, I've decided to order the army to..." at this Mr. Lincoln looked again at his rough draft, "recognize and maintain the freedom of these people." He put the paper back in his inner pocket. He gave his counselors a firm stare. "Gentlemen, we will control all that land again, and we will free those people!"

Chapter 5

And then suddenly, as John Hay prophesied, things turned upside down. There was no more talk of the armies going into winter camp. The Confederates had invaded the North! General Lee had decided to cross the Potomac! Looking back, Thomas could still barely believe the strange tale that had unfolded.

Robert E. Lee decided to use the momentum of his Second Battle of Bull Run victory to keep the North reeling. He pushed his army across the Potomac River into Maryland. Lee did this for several reasons.

Some Southerners hoped that this move would allow Maryland to join the Confederacy. It was a slave-holding state after all. With Southern troops within its borders, perhaps the state legislators would vote for Maryland secession. If that happened, Washington, D.C. would be surrounded by Confederate states. Southerners wondered how old Abe Lincoln would like that?

Some hoped that a southern victory would bring the Confederacy a European ally, such as Great Britain or France. After all, most experts agreed, the colonies had won the Revolutionary War because France had given them much needed aid.

Other Southerners talked of just getting the war out of Virginia. Let the Northerners experience the horrors of war.

Robert E. Lee had another hope. The Union's congressional midterm elections were going to occur in November. If the South defeated the North right before the elections, might the voters send antiwar minded members to Congress? Perhaps those new congressmen would vote to stop the war and let the South go its own way.

So in early September, 1862, Lee had moved his forces north. On September 9, he wrote detailed instructions letting his generals know what he wanted them to do. These orders were titled Special Order 191. Each commander was to receive a copy of the orders. All made their way to the intended recipient, except for one. Incredible as it sounded, someone had wrapped the orders around three cigars. Then that someone let those cigars, and the paper holding them, fall from his possession on a Maryland roadside.

Two Union soldiers, Corporal Barton W. Mitchell and First Sergeant John M. Bloss of the 27th Indiana Volunteer Infantry, decided to take what they were sure was a well-deserved break. They plopped down next to a rail fence. As they sat, Mitchell saw the bundle. Cigars! As Sergeant Bloss searched for a match, Corporal Mitchell glanced at the papers. He saw the title *Confidential*. He stopped scanning and began reading closely. He soon realized he held Lee's battle plans in his hand! The orders were quickly forwarded up the chain of command, (no word on what happened to the cigars). When they reached the commanding general, George McClellan exclaimed, "Now I know what to do! Here is a paper with which if I cannot whip "Bobbie Lee" I will be willing to go home."

McClellan then sent the president a telegram. "I think Lee has made a gross mistake and that he will be severely punished for it...I have the plans of the Rebels and will catch them in their own trap." He also promised the president that he would "send him trophies" from the defeated Rebel army.

Other generals might have then pushed into action. McClellan, however, decided he had time enough to carefully consider the situation. He did not order an immediate action. Instead, he told his commanders "tomorrow will be fine." The army did not to move for 18 hours. During this time, Lee was informed by a Maryland citizen that McClellan had obtained his battle plans. The 18 hour delay gave Lee a chance to change his plans and move into action.

That action turned into the bloodiest day America had ever experienced. The nation reeled as they read about the Battle of Antietam, September 17, 1862. They recoiled in horror as they learned the battle caused 22,000 casualties. 22,000 casualties in a single day!

At the end of the day's fighting, General Lee looked at his losses. He came to the sad realization that his northern invasion had not worked. He had realized none of his goals. He decided to take his army back to Virginia. For his part, General McClellan decided to let Lee go. Lee's army was not destroyed; both armies were severely damaged. General McClellan wired General Halleck, "Our victory was complete. The enemy is driven back into Virginia."

McClellan also said, "Those in whose judgement I rely tell me that I fought the battle splendidly and that it was a masterpiece of art...I feel I have done all that can be asked in twice saving the country...I feel some little pride in having, with a beaten and demoralized army, defeated Lee so utterly. Well one of these days history will I trust do me justice."

Publicly, President Lincoln embraced this victory. He needed the victory. It would let him announce his Emancipation Proclamation. The North needed the victory. So the Battle of Antietam was declared a victory, the Proclamation would be issued, and Lee and the rebel army went back to Virginia.

Privately however, President Lincoln was incensed. He was beside himself. He had sent McClellan a telegram just a few days before that read, "Destroy the Rebel army, if possible." McClellan had wired him about Lee being caught in a trap. Now, 12,000 Union casualties had occurred and the General was letting the enemy escape? Where exactly were those promised trophies?

The September days passed; leaves began to hint at turning, and there was a chance that summer might be releasing its fierce grip. Summers in D.C. were legendarily tough, so no one was taking anything for granted. Personally, Jacob had become convinced a Washington, D.C. summer could last into December, if it had a mind to.

Thomas was huddled over his desk one afternoon when Jacob came into the room. "Mr. Henderson, may I ask a question?"

Thomas straightened up, looking at his young friend. "Of course," he replied.

"Did we win the battle of Antietam?"

"What? Well, yes, of course we did. Didn't Mr. Lincoln proclaim it so?"

"Oh, well, I was just wondering."

"Just wondering? What kind of a question is that?"

"Seeing as Lee's army escaped after we had their orders and their plans all laid out…"

Thomas interrupted his young charge. "The Rebels were driven from the field. We held the battlefield when it was all over."

"Well, seeing as we had more casualties than the Rebels did…"

"Both sides inflicted horrible casualties on each other. Bloodiest day in American history!"

"Seeing as it didn't seem to settle or change one thing, I just wondered really if anyone won that battle."

Though he had publicly proclaimed it a Union win, privately Mr. Lincoln was wondering the same thing. Then the president heard a disturbing rumor. He was told that an officer, an officer on General Halleck's staff, had stated it was not the policy of the Army of the Potomac to defeat the Confederate Army in battle. Major John J. Key, a judge advocate on General Halleck's staff, had been asked why the

Army of the Potomac didn't "bag the whole Rebel army after the battle of Antietam?"

Key answered, "That is not the game…the object is that neither army shall get much advantage over the other; that both shall be kept in the field till they are exhausted, when we will make a compromise and save slavery."

As soon as he finished reading the report, President Lincoln called, "Mr. Hay! This will not do! We need to investigate this immediately. Is this one man's opinion or the opinion of all the officers of the Army of the Potomac? Did he indeed even utter these words? I understand his brother is an advisor to General McClellan. How many others feel this way? We need to get to the bottom of this!" Lincoln the lawyer went into action.

On September 26, President Lincoln sent a letter asking Key directly if the report was true. Key did not deny the quote. Then President Lincoln wrote, "In my view it is wholly inadmissible for any gentleman holding a military commission from the United States to utter such sentiments as Major Key… therefore let Major John J. Key be forthwith dismissed from the Military service of the United States."

The president knew that Key was but one man. What he really needed to know was how many others shared Key's thoughts? He needed more information before he could act. To get information, Mr. Lincoln decided to pay the Army of the Potomac and its commander a visit. He also decided to arrive unannounced.

But Mr. Lincoln found out, again, that it was virtually impossible to keep a secret in Washington, D.C. Someone slipped a word into McClellan's ear about the secret presidential visit. The general rode out and met the president at Harper's Ferry, Virginia. They then rode to the battleground. The battle was just barely two weeks past. President Lincoln looked at the scarred landscape. He saw the freshly dug graves. He saw Farmer Miller's slashed cornfields, those cornstalks that had been cut down by waves of bullets. He saw the Dunker Church, a church built by pacifists that had become a central point of the battle. Though it was two weeks after the battle, wounded troops still lay in makeshift hospitals in the area. Mr. Lincoln visited the hospitals offering comfort to both Rebel and Union soldiers.

He also spoke repeatedly with General McClellan. He urged the general to push south quickly and engage the enemy. McClellan replied "that it was most impossible of course at the present time". The general presented the president with a litany of reasons why he could not possibly move. He needed supplies, men, horses, etc. Mr. Lincoln could only shake his head in frustration. Nothing he seemed to say moved the man.

Early one morning, President Lincoln summoned his friend Oziah M. Hatch. "Come, Hatch, I want you to take a walk with me." The two walked among the pitched tents, past the sleeping soldiers, watching the dawn break over the Maryland countryside. Lincoln broke the quiet. "Do you know what this is?" he asked Hatch.

Hatch was surprised and confused by the question. "Why it is the Army of the Potomac," he answered.

"So called," Lincoln replied shaking his head, "but that is a mistake. It is only McClellan's bodyguard."

After that early morning walk, Lincoln and McClellan had no more substantive conversations.

Soon after that walk, Mr. Lincoln left the army and returned to the capital. Once there he took pen in hand and wrote his commanding general a letter. In it, he asked, "You remember when we discussed you being overcautious. Are you not being cautious when you assume you cannot do what the enemy is constantly doing? Should you not claim to be at least his equal?" The president consulted with his General in Chief, Henry Halleck. But Halleck was as disappointed with McClellan as Lincoln was. "If I could only get General McClellan to move," Halleck lamented. "He has now lain still twenty days since the battle of Antietam, and I cannot persuade him to move."

McClellan gave the president and general in chief plenty of reasons he could not move. He forwarded one report from a cavalry colonel who said his horses were absolutely unable to leave camp. A frustrated Lincoln responded, "I have just read your dispatch about sore-tongued and fatigued horses. Will you pardon me for asking what the horses of your army have done since the Battle of Antietam that fatigues anything?"

Finally on October 6, 1862, President Lincoln put it as plainly as he could. He ordered Halleck to send a direct order to General McClellan. "The President directs you cross the Potomac and give battle to the enemy or drive him south." McClellan didn't move.

Chapter 6

On an especially pleasant afternoon, the temperatures were tolerable for a change, Jacob was walking past Mr. Lincoln's office. The door was open. As he moved past the open door, he heard his name called.

Jacob pivoted in mid-stride heading back toward the open door. "Yes sir?" he answered, peering into the office. He saw the president perched on the edge of a chair with a newspaper sheet spread on the floor at his feet. He held a knife in his right hand and a small piece of lumber in his left. The paper held a small pile of wood shavings.The president smiled and beckoned Jacob into the office.

"Afternoon, Jacob. I was just wondering, back home in Indiana, did you ever do any whittlin'?"

Jacob started nodding energetically. "Oh yes sir, I had a fine knife. It came from my pa's store."

"Do you have one now?"

"Yes sir." He reached into his pocket and pulled out a brass and horn-handled pocket knife.

Mr. Lincoln nodded at a chair and offered the boy a piece of kindling. Jacob instantly accepted and started adding to the president's pile.

"Ah yes, I remember you said your father had a store. You know, I worked in a store once."

"You did, sir? Didn't know that. In Indiana?"

"No, this was later, when I was living in Illinois. Worked for a man named Denton Offutt in New Salem, Illinois."

"Did you like it, sir?"

"Well, I was glad to take the job but it turned out to be not that much of a going concern. What about you? You help out in your pa's store?"

"Oh yes sir, sweeping and such. Working with stock and shelving. I liked it." He paused as he considered, "Well, I liked it better than working on the farm anyways."

Mr. Lincoln laughed at that. "Given that choice, I agree wholeheartedly. I put my time in the fields. We grew wheat, oats, pumpkins, tobacco, and flax; we'd grow pretty much anything we could that we could eat, use, or trade. After all that, I can attest that farming is a hard life!"

"Oh yes sir, it most certainly is!" Jacob agreed.

Then Mr. Lincoln's knife paused, and he looked at Jacob, "Do you miss Indiana Jacob?"

Jacob's knife paused as well. He took a small minute before answering "Yes sir, I have to say that I do. Everyday I miss my ma, pa, and sis." Jacob ducked his head a bit as he answered. He busied himself reaching for a handkerchief and gave a small sound. A cough? He shook his head and looked up. "But I really am glad to be here and I most sincerely appreciate all that has been given to me."

Mr. Lincoln gave a reassuring wave of his hand. "Of course you do, Jacob, of course you do. But that doesn't mean, and it shouldn't mean, that you don't miss what you had before. You know, like you, I had hard times and good times in Indiana. I think you know my ma passed when I was only nine."

Jacob nodded.

"Like yours, she died of a sickness." Changing the subject, Mr. Lincoln asked, "Did you go to school?"

"Yes sir, right there in Salem. And my ma and pa gave me lessons. They taught me to read and write and figure. That helped with working in the store. Did you go to school, sir"

"In a manner of speaking. I went to blab schools for short bits and pieces. I guess you could say I went to school by littles."

Jacob gave the president a puzzled look. "Blab school?"

"Oh yes, you see a passel of us young un's of all different ages, would gather in the one-room schoolhouse. There was a teacher, one of mine was named Azel Dorsey, who was attempting to teach us all reading, writing, and penmanship. So to see how we were doing, Mr. Dorsey would have us read or recite all at the same time. Don't really know how he heard too much of anything out of all that caterwauling."

Jacob laughed at the image. Then he asked, "Where exactly did you live, sir?"

"Well, when we crossed the Ohio from Kentucky, it was called Hurricane Township, Perry County, Indiana. Later it was renamed and became part of Spencer County. I reckon we were about oh seventy or eighty-so miles southwest of you there in Salem." Mr. Lincoln pointed his piece of wood at Jacob. "I never visited Salem, it's a nice place?"

"Oh yes, sir."

Mr. Lincoln paused, "You know Jacob, as I said there were hard times but Indiana is good country."

"Yes, sir," Jacob enthusiastically agreed, "It sure is."

"Would you like to go see it again?"

That question surprised Jacob. To be honest, he hadn't thought much about. It didn't seem likely in the short term. "Uhmm, sometime, sure."

Mr. Lincoln put aside his whittling. "Well, that's good to know."

Jacob was confused "Sir?"

"Oh, nothing Jacob, just a little project I'm considering." The president unbent his tall frame. "Well, I guess I've done enough woolgathering. Best be getting back to work. Thanks for stopping, Jacob. I've enjoyed our chat." Mr. Lincoln began gathering up their wood shavings.

"Oh thank you Mr. President." As he left the room, a rather puzzled Jacob thought *"Now, I wonder what that was all about?"*

A few hours later, Thomas was wondering the exact same thing. He'd received a summons to visit the president's office.

"Ah, Thomas, thank you for coming."

"But of course, sir." Thomas answered.

"Let me come straight to it. My understanding is that you compiled a list of names for my young friend, Mr. Hay. Is that so?"

"Hmmmm," thought Thomas. He had agreed with John Hay that they hadn't needed to disturb the president with this effort, but here he was now, asking the direct question.

Thomas had no choice. "Uhm, well yes sir that is true."

Mr. Lincoln gave Thomas a piercing look. "May I see that list please?"

"I'll be happy to fetch it, sir."

"Please do. And now if you would."

"Yes sir." Thomas began rapidly walking toward his desk. A few minutes later he was handing the president his work. Mr. Lincoln glanced at the document, folded it lengthwise and placed it in the inner pocket of his suit coat. He patted the outside of the pocket and said, "Thank you son. It gives me something to work with." Nodding to Thomas but not saying another word, the president left the office. Thomas was left standing in the president's office wondering, *"Now what was that all about?"* It was apparent that the president was considering something.

It seemed that everyone in the capital wondered what the president would do next. Being Washington, D.C., rumors soon started flying. McClellan was in trouble! Little Mac supporters began reading their tea leaves and peering into their crystal balls. They did not like what they saw and began pressuring Lincoln. They gave him reason after reason why Little Mac was "The One" to lead the army. Lincoln listened patiently, but when they finished, he rebutted their arguments.

"Gentlemen, I have said it before, I will say it: for organizing an army, for preparing an army for the field, for fighting a defensive campaign, I will back General McClellan against any general of modern times. I don't know but of ancient times, either." He swept his eyes around the room before continuing. "But, gentlemen, the man is not a fighter. He has no heart for it. He has proved that. The Peninsula Campaign proved that. Antietam proved that. In Virginia he was sitting at the very edge of Richmond and was driven away by what I believe was a smaller force. Still, I gave him a second chance. I brought him back after Second Bull Run and gave him specific orders. Destroy the Rebel army if possible. Antietam gave him his chance to do that.

McClellan had received the gift of the Lost Special Order 191. Why as soon as he read that, he promised that if he could not whip Bobby Lee, he would be willing to go home. He had promised to deliver trophies from the vanquished army. Instead of delivering trophies, he had let the Rebels slide right back to Virginia. True the rebels were bloodied, but the Army of the Potomac received more casualties." His voice rose a notch. "And while receiving those casualties, he kept two fresh corps, Porter's V and Franklins VI in reserve. In a battle so closely contested, those men never saw action. They never saw the field. Afterwards, the commanding general announced that he saw this battle as brilliant." Lincoln looked at his listeners, as if asking, 'Can you believe that?'

"I then directly ordered him to move. It took him nineteen days before he put a man over the Potomac River. It took him nine more days to finish the move. Then he stopped again, delaying on little pretexts of wanting this and that. I began to fear he was playing false – that he did not want to hurt the enemy." Lincoln gave the group a steely look. "Well gentlemen, that will not do. We need to subdue the Rebel army and reestablish the Union. Letting the enemy slip away will not do."

Francis P. Blair Sr., a man Lincoln respected, mounted a last gasp try to save McClellan. He tried to convince the president that the general should stay. Blair made his case and Lincoln listened, but finally the president said, "I have tried long enough to bore with an auger too dull to take hold. I said I would remove him if he let Lee's army get away from him, and I must do so. He has got the *'slows,'* Mr. Blair, *'the slows'*.

In another White House office, Jacob also was grappling with an issue. He sat in John Hay's office sorting mail and messages. Thomas had given Jacob a large stack to deliver to Mr. Hay and now he was helping Hay sort through the stack. Jacob liked John Hay and he liked spending time with him. It might have been because they were both Indiana born. It might also have been because Mr. Hay made him laugh.

"Mr. Hay," Jacob began, "Can I, uhmm, I mean may I ask you a question?"

Hunched over his desk, John Hay offered a grunt as his answer. His attention remained on the message he was reading.

"Do you think Major Key was a traitor?"

"Hmmm," came the reply.

"Did he set out to help the Rebels win?" Jacob continued.

"Hmmm," Hay said again. Then he apparently really heard Jacob's question and turned toward the young man. "Wait, no, what? What did you ask?"

"I asked if you thought Major Key was a traitor?"

"No!" Hay answered quickly, "at least not really, I guess," he continued in a slower tone. "Well, I guess I need to know what do you mean by traitor?"

Now it was Jacob's turn to be a bit confused.

"Uhm, well, you know a turncoat, a Benedict Arnold."

"Ah well, if that is your question, then my answer is no, Major Key was not acting as a traitor."

"Why not? I mean why do you say that?"

"If I am interpreting your definition correctly, I do not equate Major Key with General Arnold. I believe Benedict Arnold wanted the Americans to lose. I think he wanted the British to take command of West Point. I don't believe Major Key wanted the Rebels to win the war."

"But he said, I think this is right, that 'the game wasn't to bag the Rebels.' Isn't that wanting them to win?"

"Now I may be wrong, I freely admit. I am putting meaning in another man's word and there is always danger in that. But I believe Major Key wants the Union to be preserved. I think he just wants to return to the status quo of 1860. One country, part free, part slave. I don't think he wants the Union torn apart."

"But I don't understand. He's a Union officer. He serves Mr. Lincoln and he should support the president's plans, should follow his orders."

"Ah yes, the *'he shoulds'*." Hay said. "Do you remember when we had the discussion about military generals and political ones?"

"Yes, sir."

"Well, along that same vein we have Northern officers and then we have Northern officers."

Jacob was clearly confused by that answer.

Hay laughed, "I know, I know I seem to be making no sense. But what I mean is we have officers who wear the Union uniform who support Mr. Lincoln and follow his every order. But we also have officers serving who feel they know better than Mr. Lincoln. They feel they have more military experience, more military training, and knowledge. So they may question his orders or drag their feet while they follow them.

Others feel that while they support the cause, they must also never lose sight of the very important job of supporting and advancing themselves."

Jacob shook his head irritably at this line of reasoning. "Fine! I'll just admit it; I don't know what you're saying."

"It is a peculiar situation, I admit. Let me try again, some officers joined and fight but they also keep an eye firmly on their own future. You must remember that not everyone supported Mr. Lincoln in

1860; not everyone will support him in 1862 or in 1864."

"What?!" a very surprised Jacob said, "why of course they will! There's a war on!"

"Oh, there's a war on alright," Hay quickly agreed, "but some people have their eyes firmly fixed on their own futures. For some, it's how much credit do they get for helping win the war? What future benefit will they receive? How can they turn their efforts into profits? They want to win because they want to advance themselves. They need to shine that light brightly on themselves so they can prosper at war's end.

And for others, it's a constant eye on the calendar. After all, midterm elections are coming soon, and 1864 is only 24 months after that."

"1864?" Jacob said.

"Yes, the next presidential election. The beauty of American democracy is that there is always an election no more than two years away and a chance to select a president every four. We selected Abraham Lincoln in 1860. Who knows what will happen in 1864?"

"Why I do!" Jacob indignantly insisted. "Mr. Lincoln will be reelected. No one would dare run against him!"

"My dear young man, they are running against him as we speak!"

Jacob was shocked. "Who would dare?"

John laughed. "Why some of the same men who ran against him in 1860. Think back. The Republicans had the chance to nominate Senator William Seward, or they could have nominated Governor Salmon P. Chase, Senator Simon Cameron, former representative Edward Bates, or Senator Wade. Of course we now know them as Secretary of State Seward, Secretary of War Cameron, Secretary of Treasury Salmon Chase and Attorney General Bates."

Jacob leaned far back in his chair considering the situation. Truth be told he hadn't been paying that much attention to the political situation two years ago. These men ran against the president and now sat in his Cabinet? And some were considering another run against him?

"There are sitting cabinet members who are going to run against Mr. Lincoln for president in 1864?" he asked incredulously.

"Let me say there are current Cabinet members who want to be president in 1864." John Hay amended.

"Well I never!" said Jacob.

"Ah the wonderful world of politics. Welcome to Washington, Jacob."

Chapter 7

Thomas walked into their Dodge House rooms early one evening waving a telegram. He was obviously agitated. "I knew this would happen!" He shook his head, "I knew this would happen!" he repeated. He was speaking rapidly. "I just didn't know when. Oh, I was really hoping to avoid this, but I suppose I was deluding myself."

Jacob was putting food stuffs away hoping to hasten the arrival of the evening meal. "What's that Mr. Henderson?" asked Jacob in a slightly muffled voice. He was bent over, head deep in their pantry.

Thomas waved the telegram again. "My father is coming; he's coming here."

"Your father is coming to Washington City?" Jacob asked, pulling away from the pantry. "Is that bad news?"

"Well no, of course not. It's not precisely bad news; no, it's not bad at all, I mean it just means…well, I'm not sure what it means." Thomas had begun circling their table as he talked. "It could mean many things."

Jacob didn't really understand, but he nodded his head nonetheless. This was something he wasn't going to get involved in if he could help it.

"Fine then," Thomas finally concluded. "First thing, day after tomorrow, he'll be coming into the Baltimore and Ohio Train Depot. First thing. Thursday morning, 8 a.m. sharp! Yes sir!"

Thomas hadn't seen his parents in months. In fact, he'd pretty much been away from the family for over two years. There had been short trips back up to New York City, of course. In fact, Thomas had taken the train up to the city right after he'd accepted Mr. Lincoln's offer to work in the Lincoln administration. But he'd kept those visits short, pleading work pressures. Now, the situation had changed. It appeared Muhammad was coming to the mountain. Thomas was not ready for this.

Thomas loved his family, he truly did. And he knew, beyond doubt that they loved him. They supported him. They had paid for his college education at the College of William and Mary. They continued to support him with monthly stipends. They had told him they were proud of his efforts to help preserve the Union. They still bragged to their friends about his White House job. But Thomas always had a worry. Every male in his family had gone into some part of the field of medicine. His father was a well respected physician and surgeon at Bellevue Hospital in New York City. Thomas was fully expected to follow their leads.

The only problem was that Thomas had no intention of making that journey. He wasn't exactly sure what he wanted to do with his life, but he knew it was not medicine. That was not a conversation he looked forward to having with his father. And Thomas assumed that was the purpose of his father's journey. Why else would he be leaving his family and his work in New York City to travel all the way down to Washington, D.C.?

Thursday, October 23, dawned bright and beautiful as Thomas hailed an early morning hansom. "This is not a day to be late," he proclaimed to Jacob.

The two swung into the cab as Thomas gave the driver their destination address. "New Jersey and C street, please. The B&O Depot."

The early morning traffic was relatively light and they did make it to the Baltimore and Ohio Depot on time. "Please wait, we'll be back shortly." Thomas promised the driver.

Thomas and Jacob waited as the 8 a.m. train from Baltimore pulled in, right on time. After only a few minutes of waiting, they saw Doctor Alexander Henderson. Jacob had never seen Thomas' father, but he knew who the man was the minute he saw him. Of course he was older than Thomas, but if you took away the years the two could almost pass as twins. The same tall slim build, the same wide shoulders, the same black hair, though Dr. Henderson's was streaked with grey. He had a salt and pepper beard. Jacob was stunned with the family resemblance.

"Thomas!" the man called. He approached quickly and wrapped his son in a bear hug. Then he turned to Jacob, offering his hand "Jacob, it's so nice to finally meet you. Of course, Thomas has spoken of you often."

"The pleasure is mine sir. Welcome to the capital."

Thomas reached out for his father's bag and said, "We've booked you into the Willard Hotel, Father."

"The Willard?" Doctor Henderson said with some surprise. "Now I believe that's a hotel I've heard of. Is that where you two live?"

Thomas laughed, "Oh, that's too rich for the blood of an assistant secretary, I assure you."

"We have rooms at the Dodge House," Jacob chimed in. "It's a few blocks southwest of here." He waved a hand in its general direction. "It's nice, but famous people stay at the Willard. Why, did you know President Lincoln spent his first night in the city at the Willard?"

They walked as they talked and soon emerged from the Depot. They walked past the four-sided clock tower that rose 100 feet in the air dominating the nearby skyline. They returned to their hansom. The driver hopped down to place the doctor's bags in the rack and the three piled into the cab's interior. "Willard Hotel, please driver," Thomas directed, "And please use the Massachusetts to K Street route. I'd like to arrive from the north."

Turning to his father, he explained, "That route will take us past the White House."

"A site I am very eager to see!" his father assured him.

As they made the two-mile trip, Dr. Henderson turned his attention to Jacob. "So Jacob," he said as he settled against the back of the hansom's seat. "you're from Indiana, correct?"

"Yes sir," Jacob quickly answered, "Salem, Indiana. A small town in the southern part of the state."

"Thomas has of course told us your story. So let me ask you, how's this arrangement working out? How's my son treating you?" Dr. Henderson's eyes twinkled as he asked the question.

"Oh it's working very well, sir. To tell the truth, it's perfect!"

Dr. Henderson gave a hearty laugh. "Perfect is it? Oh my…"

"Father!" Thomas admonished, in a rather dry tone. Changing the subject, he asked, "How was your journey?"

"Long and bumpy," came the quick reply. The doctor rubbed his shoulder. "Well to be honest, the only issue was changing trains in Baltimore. Outside of that, it was fine." He took a minute to watch the passing cityscape before resuming. "You know I visited this city twenty years ago, and it took me a full two days on the train to get here. Now, even with the transfer, it's a single day." He paused rubbing the other shoulder. "Still not much sleep on a bouncing train though."

"Father!" Thomas interjected. He pointed out the right-hand window. "There's the White House."

"Ah, yes." The doctor gave his full attention to the house and grounds as they rolled by.

They soon arrived at the five storied Willard, and Thomas talked to the front desk confirming that his father did indeed have a room. Then Thomas and his father agreed to meet for a late lunch. "I'll rub the road off and get a quick rest. Then we can catch up. Is that agreeable?"

"Yes sir, it is. Shall I meet you here at 12:30?"

"That will be fine."

With that, they parted. Thomas and Jacob started walking the short distance to the White House. Thomas' apprehension had rubbed off on Jacob. After all, Jacob's entire situation rested on Thomas' situation. His lodging, his job, everything. So Jacob, hesitantly spoke, "Your father seems very nice, Mr. Henderson." He hoped that would give Thomas an opening to share some information.

"Oh he is, Jacob."

"So are we all right then?"

"What do you mean?"

"Are we going to be able to continue to work and live here?"

"I most certainly hope so," an uncharacteristically solemn Thomas replied.

At 12:15 p.m., Thomas made his way into the Willard lobby. He found his father sitting in a blue patterned wing backed chair, reading a newspaper. He rose and offered his son his hand. "Shall we repair to the dining room? I find myself famished!"

They were seated at a table covered with a crisply pressed and cornered white tablecloth. The air was scented with cigar smoke. Champagne corks popped around them. Thomas and his father ordered Chesapeake oysters to start their meal.

Thomas decided to open the conversation. "It's wonderful to see you, Father. To what do I owe the honor?"

Dr. Henderson plopped an oyster in his mouth. Swallowing, he then patted his mouth with his napkin. "Can't a father merely come see his son? Do I need a reason other than that?" He smiled at Thomas. "But yes, there is another concern." He patted his mouth again with the napkin. "Son, twice, twice within a single month, Rebel armies have placed themselves between you and your mother and me. We are worried about your safety."

That answer completely surprised Thomas. He was certain the medical career would be the first topic of conversation. But his physical well-being? Of course there was a war going on, but not once since he taken the job, had he considered himself in danger.

But of course, he instantly took his parents' point. He lived in Washington City, they lived in New York City, some two hundred miles to the north. He could most certainly understand how his parents could be worried. Of course there had been the Battle of Antietam in Maryland. Then on October 9, less than a month later, Confederate General J.E.B. Stuart had crossed the Potomac and moved 1800 men into Chambersburg, Pennsylvania. His men cut telegraph wires, seized horses and carried away all they could. What they couldn't carry away, they tried to destroy. The Confederates had crossed back into Virginia three days later. Union forces gathered to try to defend, but the deed was done. Once again, Stuart had ridden into or around Northern forces and made it appear the North could do nothing to stop him. He terrorized, stole, destroyed, and lost but one man in the effort.

Dr. Henderson continued, "Your mother's worried, I'm worried. This war is lasting far longer than we thought, or hoped that it would. The first time, when Lee invaded Maryland, was bad enough. But the second time when Stuart invaded Pennsylvania, well, that tipped the tide. We made the decision I should come down and talk with you."

Thomas nodded.

"So let me ask you, Son," he looked directly in Thomas' eyes, "How are you?"

Thomas knew that question held several layers. Mirroring his father, he took an oyster to gain time as he marshaled his thoughts. He also tapped the edge of his mouth with his white linen napkin.

"Sir, first of all, let me assure you, I am fine. Let me also say I can fully understand your and Mother's position. I can understand your apprehension, your concerns. I understand I live in the midst of a war-torn nation." He took a deep breath before continuing. "But I have to tell you truthfully, sir, I was surprised by your comment. I do not consider myself in any more risk than anyone else in the nation. Perhaps, working at the White House, even less." He paused to look at his father, but spoke quickly before his father could respond. "Now I have been at risk, and I have felt terror. Last June in Manassas scared me to death and scarred me for life. No doubt." An image of a boot spinning through the air suddenly reappeared in his mind. When he had seen the boot last June, it had still carried its owners leg. Thomas gave his head a little shake. "But I do not feel that way now," he paused again, "with all due respect, sir."

Dr. Henderson let his son continue. "I know the war has not gone well for us, and it certainly has lasted longer than I thought it would."

"Amen to that!" Dr. Henderson said. "Remember all those fools, let me get 'jined up' before the fun ends?

Let me get into battle because the war will only last one battle? Nincompoops! Idiots!"

"Yes sir," Thomas agreed "but I do believe things are improving. I'm not willing to say we're turning the tide but I do sense a change."

"Let me ask it plainly. " Dr. Henderson pointed his fork directly at his son. "I take it you are not ready to come back to New York and resume your collegiate career at Columbia?" He gave his son a hopeful look as he lowered the fork.

Thomas took another deep breath. "No sir, not at this time." He gently lifted his hand half way toward his father as he continued. "Mr. Lincoln has told me I am helping him and helping the war effort. As long as I can do that, I feel compelled to do so. I hope you understand, sir." Thomas most certainly hoped his father would accept this line of reasoning and not press on "the medical issue".

Dr. Henderson reached out and placed his hand on his son's arm. "I have to say I thought this would be your answer. Your mother and I selfishly want you home in New York, safely tucked away, but we do understand. The Union must be preserved, and we do understand that you are helping in that effort. We won't pressure you to come home."

The doctor leaned back in his chair, "But I wish I was more sanguine about the outcome of the war."

Thomas jumped on this. "Well sir, I have an idea. I suggest we move from this subject and talk of life in New York and Washington City. Let's enjoy an excellent luncheon and then I think I can provide you with some more information concerning the war. What say you, sir, to this course of action?"

Dr. Henderson leaned back in his chair, looked at his son and gave his agreement. "Capital! Yes, sir. I accept your plan!" And that's what they did. They enjoyed an excellent lunch. Thomas asked for all the gossip from New York. Of course, he did not call it that - he asked for the news of the day. His father wanted to hear all about life in the nation's capital.

When they completed what was indeed an excellent lunch, Thomas led his father up Pennsylvania Avenue. He intended to give his father the complete nickel tour.

Like many others, Dr. Henderson was amazed that private citizens could just walk right up to and through the White House doors. Unlike private citizens who walked in and muddled about, Thomas knew exactly where he was going. He led his father to his "space".

As they walked the White House halls, Dr. Henderson swung his head right to left, trying to see everything. He was in awe. "Truly impressive, Thomas! And to think you work here and help with the war effort."

Thomas hoped he had not stretched that "helping with the war effort" line.

The two swung into what Thomas had begun to think of as his cranny. Jacob was seated. He quickly jumped up when he saw them. "Dr. Henderson," he said smiling "Welcome to our world." He bowed as he welcomed the doctor.

Dr. Henderson looked around the space being careful not to hit his head on the sloped ceiling. Others might have looked down their nose at the small space, but the doctor looked genuinely impressed.

"So tell me gentlemen, what is it precisely you do here? Thomas?"

"Well sir, I am an assistant secretary to the president. My first job is to examine the overnight reports, evaluate their contents, and send them on to the appropriate people. My second job is to research and write for Mr. Lincoln's staff, including…well including Mr. Lincoln. And of course, I do anything I can to help Mr. Lincoln's secretaries, John Nicolay and John Hay."

"Goodness," the doctor said. "And you, Jacob?"

"Me?" Jacob stopped to think for a second. "Well, whatever they ask!"

Thomas and his father both laughed.

"Jacob is officially an assistant to the assistant secretary of the president." Thomas told his father. "Unofficially, he does all sorts of things around here. He's a real help."

Jacob smiled, "As I told you sir, it's perfect."

Then both Thomas and Jacob simultaneously turned to look at the door. They had recognized the familiar distinctive tread of their employer coming down the hall.

"Good afternoon, gentlemen." said President Lincoln as he entered the room. "Thomas, I understand we have a visitor." He, too, was careful not to knock his head on the low ceiling.

"Yes sir, we do. President Lincoln, I have the honor of presenting my father, Dr. Alexander Henderson of New York City."

Mr. Lincoln extended his hand to Dr. Henderson. "So very good to meet you Dr. Henderson. Your son is quite an asset. He's doing a very good job helping me in my efforts." A broad grin grew as Mr. Lincoln turned "As is, of course, his very capable assistant, Mr. Bunten. Why Jacob can accomplish practically anything!" The men laughed while Jacob puffed up.

"Mr. President, what an honor!" said Dr. Henderson. "I cannot believe I am actually meeting you. What a privilege." He paused. "May I thank you for all you are doing to save the country? We appreciate it so much!"

Mr. Lincoln gave a solemn nod. "I am doing my best to uphold my oath to protect the Constitution and this country. If we are having any success, I must give the credit to God above, the soldiers, my staff, and to people such as you Dr. Henderson, supporters of this great Union."

Then, exhibiting what Thomas was starting to think of as the Lincoln grin, he turned to Jacob.

"Now Jacob, I always welcome pleasant news. Did I hear you say something was perfect?"

"Oh yes sir, I was telling Dr. Henderson that working here was perfect for me."

"Perfect hey? Well that reminds me of a story I heard back in Illinois. A preacher was telling the congregation, during his sermon, that the Lord was the only perfect man and the Bible never mentions a perfect woman. A woman in the rear of the congregation called out, 'I know a perfect woman, and I've heard of her every day for the last six years.'

"Who was she?" asked the surprised minister.

"My husband's first wife," came the reply."

As he finished, Mr. Lincoln guffawed, Thomas and his father joined him. Jacob smiled politely but seemed confused.

Then Mr. Lincoln turned his attention back to Dr. Henderson. " I hear remarkable things about that addition to your hospital in New York, Dr. Henderson. Bellevue isn't it? And you've added a teaching hospital?"

Dr. Henderson looked surprised but happy. "Yes sir, it is a medical college associated with the hospital. We've been open about a year now."

"Marvelous!" said the president. "The strides we are making these days!" He moved to another subject. "How long can you stay with us, Doctor?"

"I'd like to stay three or four days, if possible, sir."

"If there is anything I can do, please don't hesitate to let me know. As Thomas will tell you, the White House door is open. Gentlemen, it has been a pleasure, but duty calls. Doctor Henderson," he said, extending his hand, "my pleasure."

"Oh, the pleasure is all mine, Mr. President, let me assure you."

When the president had gone, Dr. Henderson could barely contain his excitement. "To actually meet the president…and for him to know about our medical school!"

Thomas and Jacob smiled. They were just a bit more used to the "Lincoln Magic".

Dr. Henderson told the president he hoped to stay three or four days. He stayed six. He loved the time he spent with his son and he enjoyed seeing the city. He visited the White House every day. Thomas took him to the War Department where they caught a glimpse of the president conferring with Secretary Stanton. Each day, Dr. Henderson saw more and more of Thomas' world. He came to understand more about the job his son was doing.

They also enjoyed the time off the president extended to both Thomas and Jacob. They walked the city, visiting a variety of sites, including the Smithsonian, which truly impressed the good doctor. They also enjoyed the new horse-driven street cars. They ate well, visiting the Old Ebbitt Grill and once even made their way out to Potomac, Maryland, where they dined at the Old Angler's Mill.

The good doctor came to see that his son was not in imminent danger. Thomas took him to see some of the city's defenses. Thomas made sure his father knew that there were over fifty strongly-defended forts in the area. He took him past miles of rifle pits. He made sure his father saw the cannons that stood ready to repel the Rebel assault. He saw the hundreds of troops that walked the streets of the city. Dr. Henderson did begin to believe that his son was about as safe as he could be, given he lived in the middle of the war. Dr. Henderson made one more half-hearted pitch for a move home to New York, but he knew he would make no progress. "Well then, visit home soon and see your Mother. She worries and misses you so. And Jacob you must come as well. We would love to have you stay with us. We'll show you New York City."

"I'd like that sir."

Dr. Henderson left Washington, D.C. reassured. Things seemed to be in hand.

Had he waited but a few more days, Dr. Henderson could have been in the capital when Mr. Lincoln proved things were not well in hand. He could have been present when the president stunned the capital by making the following announcement: "By direction of the president it is ordered that Major General McClellan be relieved from the command of the Army of the Potomac: and that Major General Burnside take the command of that army."

Chapter 8

"Who is General Burnsides, anyway?" Jacob asked.

"What!" exclaimed John Hay. "And you say you're from Indiana!"

"And it's General Burnside, not Burnsides," corrected John Nicolay.

"What's Indiana got to do with it?" Jacob asked as he glared at them both.

"He was born in Indiana." said Nicolay.

"Liberty, Indiana to be precise." added Hay. The three were in Nicolay's office, right next door to the president's office, discussing the news of the day.

Jacob continued his glare, "I *am* from Indiana! And it's a big state, you know, with a lot of people. You can't expect a body to know all of them!"

Nicolay ignored Jacob's comments, "General Ambrose Burnsides is a commander in the Army of the Potomac. He was the commander of the North Carolina campaign which was very successful, and he's served under McClellan in the Peninsula Campaign and at the Battle of Antietam."

"Humph," Jacob gave a little snort. "not sure those last two would qualify you for a promotion."

"Now, now, Jacob," admonished Hay. "None of that. And you do know Burnside, at least to look at. He's the general with that fancy fluffy half beard…"

"I believe they are now calling the style sideburns," said Nicolay.

Recognition came to Jacob. The man did have distinctive facial hair. "Oh him? He's the new commander? Hmmph. Well, alright then. But now I have another question. I know for a first-hand fist hard fact that previously, once, if not twice, the president decided the army would not stand for the firing of McClellan. Why did he feel free to do it now? What has changed?"

John Nicolay answered first, "I think, Jacob, that Jupiter has…"

"Jupiter?" Jacob interrupted.

John Hay laughed. "Oh, you'll have to forgive John, Jacob. He sometimes refers to Mr. Lincoln as Jupiter. You know the king of the Roman gods, the god of thunder and lightning."

"I'm not alone in the usage!" Nicolay quickly broke in.

"True enough!" Hay agreed.

"Anyway, as I was saying, I believe the president senses that many of the men have reevaluated McClellan. To be sure, they see him as their protector, as a great trainer and teacher, but I think, I sense, they have come, or at least many of them have come to see him as an ineffectual battlefield general."

Hay added, "I think they love him, but they're are no longer sure he's the one to lead them to victory. Oh, there will always be McClellan supporters, but I think the majority of the fighting men are ready for a change."

Thomas walked into the room. "So he's done it." It wasn't a question.

"Without a doubt," John Hay replied. "It's fait accompli."

Nicolay said, "Fait accompli perhaps, but for how long?"

"Excellent point, my dear Mr. Nicolay."

"Now what in tarnation does that mean?" asked Jacob.

Thomas said, "Fait accompli means the deed is done."

"And I mean," John Hay said waving his hands in a circular motion, "that as I gaze into my crystal ball, I don't see our dear General Burnside staying long in command."

"What makes you say that?"

"A little bit of inside knowledge. I know that Burnside himself turned the command down twice. Said he wasn't up to it. Then when he was ordered to accept the other day, he spent two hours trying to talk his way out of command."

"The way I hear it," Nicolay offered, "the only reason he accepted is that they told him General Hooker was the next choice and Burnside supposedly hates Hooker."

"Pretty poor reason to accept command!" Thomas snapped.

"Which is why, Thomas, I need you to return to that report you created for me."

"The one the president currently has?"

"That's the one," said Hay, evidently unabashed. Neither of them knew if that list had played any role in the president's decision.

"Your original list was very good, Thomas, but I feel we need to expand the list. Previously, we restricted the list to generals in the East. This time, please include generals from the West. And please pay special attention to one man - General U.S. Grant. I believe you know the name." he finished dryly.

"General U.S. Grant," Thomas affirmed, "Yes sir..." he looked up at Hay. "I mean yes John."

Nicolay changed the subject, "Jacob, Thomas, you are both out talking with civilians and soldiers. How is the Emancipation being received?"

Jacob and Thomas looked at one another. Jacob decided to let Thomas have first crack at this question. "I guess about what you'd expect, John. Some folks agree; some are pretty upset about it. And there are a lot of questions about it."

"It's so confusing!!" Jacob jumped in. "I mean, does it free the slaves or not?"

"Perhaps it's more complicated than it is confusing." John Hay responded. "Remember how we talked previously about political generals and military generals? Well, this issue has some similar aspects. Some people want to see it as a moral issue. They focus on the evils of slavery, but we cannot see it that way. The constitution allows slavery. Until it's changed..."

"But," Nicolay interrupted, "those rebelling states say the Constitution no longer has any power over them. I do love the hypocrisy. Did you know a Confederate officer approached General Butler under a flag of truce to demand that his slaves be returned? Seems they'd run away and were seeking sanctuary with our troops at Fort Monroe. He demanded that General Butler obey the laws of the country, specifically the Fugitive Slave Law and return his property. General Butler calmly told him that law was passed by the United States Congress and applied to U.S. citizens. Was the rebelling officer ending his rebellion and coming back into the Union? Needless to say, he did not get his slaves back."

"Oh," John Hay laughed, "you can clearly see General Butler is a lawyer."

Nicolay laughed as well. "When the first escaped slaves made their way into Fort Monroe, no one knew exactly what to do with them. People weren't sure of their legal status. Then General Butler made his decision. He said it was not a moral decision but a military one. Before the war, Butler was a pro South Democrat. Why in 1860, he wanted the Democrats to nominate Jefferson Davis for president instead of Stephen Douglas!"

"But he also knew that if he returned those slaves to their masters, they would be sent back to do work that was helping the Southern war effort. They'd work on entrenchments, work in factories, work on farms freeing up white men to serve as soldiers. Slaves even help the army in the field. They cook for them, and dig their trenches. In General

Butler's opinion, every slave that was removed from Southern control, caused a job to go undone or a soldier to leave the battlefield and return to work. Butler claimed that his effort was not a moral one, but a war-shortening one and everyone should be in favor of that!"

"But," John Hay jumped in, "it also explains why not all slaves were freed. If we take the position that we are allowed to take the property of Rebels because that helps with the war effort, we cannot touch the slaves in the states that are not rebelling."

"Missouri, Kentucky, Maryland and Delaware," Thomas listed.

"Exactly! They stayed in the Union, and the Constitution does apply to them. And until it is changed, the Constitution says slavery is legal in the United States. So Mr. Lincoln could not include their slaves in the Emancipation Proclamation."

"And then add in the geography issue."

"How's that?" Jacob asked.

"Remember the president's order applies to places that our forces control. There are a lot of places we don't control yet, as you very well know."

Jacob threw his hands up in the air. "What a rat's nest!" he exclaimed.

"Oh, without a doubt, a bigger rat's nest than you know, Jacob. But don't lose sight of the fact that the majority of slaves, the vast majority in fact, will be freed. We will win this war and we will control all the South!"

Jacob looked at John Hay intently for a minute. Then he said, "And when we do, do you know what that will mean?" He paused, "It will mean freedom will follow *our* flag."

Strong words. But those words that did not look like they would becoming true anytime soon in the early days of November, 1862. True enough, Lee had been forced to retreat from Maryland, but his string of victories outnumbered his defeats. There was still a strong Southern army in the field rebelling against the United States. The Southern leadership appeared to be getting stronger by the day. Mr. Lincoln was still searching for a commander for his army.

Thomas devoted his time to working on that search. He went back to researching the subject. Though his list was not that old, major changes had to be made. Thomas felt a spasm of pain as he looked at the name that topped his first list. General Philip Kearny. Thomas could still not quite believe he was gone.

Other names had to be crossed off as well.
Some had tried and failed, Pope for one. Some had
run counter to the administration's policies, Fremont.
Some were too close to McClellan, Fitz John Porter.
There were still strong candidates, John Reynolds of
Pennsylvania for instance, but the list was getting
smaller. Thomas was glad to expand the list
westward.

If you were sitting in the nation's capital in
1862, it was easy to focus on the Eastern campaigns.
Robert E. Lee was in the East and his successful Rebel
army threatened the city. Those Western battles
seemed far away, somehow a bit less important. Yet
the victories the Western troops achieved were
important. Mr. Lincoln knew that the campaigns in
the West were crucial to the war's outcome.

Thomas began going through the list of
Western generals. Some names he knew, others he
was going to have to research. He did see one to add
almost immediately, John Alexander McClernand, a
general from Illinois and a strong supporter of the
war and of Mr. Lincoln. Perhaps he should lead the
list? Second would be…second would be…Thomas'
pen hung above the paper. Before writing the name
he was considering, he needed to do more research.
Too many open questions on this one.

Three days later, Thomas was back in Nicolay's office. John Hay joined them. Thomas was ready to present his list. "What do you have for us today, Thomas?" asked Nicolay.

Nicolay greatly interested Thomas. He knew that he had been born in Bavaria and immigrated to the United States. Thomas knew that he had attended school in Cincinnati and later moved to Springfield, where he met and quickly became devoted to Mr. Lincoln. In fact, Lincoln's first act as president had been to name Nicolay as his private secretary. Thomas also knew that one of John Nicolay's first acts had been to convince the president to hire John Hay. While Nicolay did not have Hay's personality, in fact some described him as dour, Thomas always found him to be a pleasant soul.

"Well s..." Thomas checked himself and gave a small grin. "Well, Johns," he emphasized the 's'.

"Oh, dear," John Hay said, "I appear to have created a monster! Sorry, Nicolay!"

Thomas just smiled and continued, "I have the list you requested. It is a rather short list." He handed the paper to John Hay, who shared it with Nicolay. "But it represents my opinions."

Hay took the offered paper and began reading. "Ohhh," he said in a surprised voice.

"Indeed!" agreed Nicolay, who was reading over Hay's shoulders. The two men shared a look.

"Fine, Thomas, you have our undivided attention," said Hay. "Now please tell us why this list starts with General U.S. Grant!"

"Well, Johns," Thomas smiled again. "I admit it came as a surprise to me as well. Starting off, we all knew though he has won battles, Grant's name has had a cloud over it."

"Indeed," agreed Nicolay again.

"But as I dug a bit deeper, I found a fair amount of dissembling. Gentlemen, I've come to the conclusion that we were not getting the truth or at least the full accurate report on General U.S. Grant!"

"Pray continue and convince us," Nicolay affably said.

"I'll not promise to convince you," Thomas said, "but here's what I've found." He consulted his notes and plunged into the subject. "We know he led the campaign to conquer Forts Henry and Donelson. And we know," he quickly added, "that the Navy played a major role in those victories, a role that Grant has not only acknowledged, but praised. He does not appear to be a glory hound. We also know his famous demand for 'Unconditional Surrender'. We know the man is a fighter."

Both Hay and Nicolay nodded but waited.

"And of course we know he won the Battle of Shiloh. Strangely, at least to me, after all that, he came away with a besmirched reputation. That did not make sense to me, so I began to dig a bit deeper. And gentlemen, I found things that did not make any sense at all. Let me give you an example. Grant captures Fort Henry and Fort Donelson and those victories help open the entire state of Tennessee to us. But when his commander reports those victories to his commander, Halleck to McClellan in this case, I found the response to be…well… let's say I found it to be off putting." Thomas pulled another paper out of his pocket. "After the battle General Halleck wired McClellan. He said and I quote, 'Give me command of the West. I ask this in return for Forts Henry and Donelson.'" Upon reading this, at first glance, it might appear General Halleck led the campaign, but he did not. He was not even there.

"Secondly, he sent another dispatch to General McClellan that read, 'Grant had won a victory at Fort Donelson but his army is as demoralized by the victory of Fort Donelson as was the Army of the Potomac by the defeat of Bull Run.' Gentlemen, I'll be blunt. That makes no sense to me."

Nicolay and Hay shared another look.

"My last point on Fort Henry and Donelson was actually provided by Mr. Dana. He told me Stanton sent him a note asking if it were not something that 'General McClellan tried to take credit for the victory, when he had communicated nothing to Grant and was 700 miles away.'"

"Now gentlemen, after the Battle of Shiloh, we heard Grant described as the Butcher. But the results of Second Bull Run and Antietam prove that was just the first of the terrible battles we're enduring. I have also learned that Halleck wrote McClellan a dispatch saying he had not heard from General Grant and that Grant was not obeying his orders. McClellan wrote back, 'Generals must observe discipline as well as private soldiers. Do not hesitate to arrest him at once if the good of the service requires it.' Now what kind of a comment is this, I ask you?

Lastly, we've heard Grant drinks. And it appears to be true, but from what I've found, his drinking was not during this war, but actually occurred between the wars. This was when he was stationed in California in 1853. It appears Halleck knew him then and formed a very unfavorable opinion of the man. That opinion seems to be coloring his current reports."

Thomas took a deep breath and laid his report on the desk. "So that is my reasoning, sirs. It may well be flawed, but it is what I currently see."

Nicolay and Hay shared one last look at each other. Then Hay spoke, "Commendable work, Thomas."

"Yeoman's work!" agreed Nicolay.

"I'm not saying I agree with it all," John Hay said, "but you've given us a great deal to consider."

"More than just consider, I think, John," said Nicolay, "I think we need to dig more deeply into this matter."

Chapter 9

Presidential Secretary John Hay proved to be prescient once again. On Sunday November 9, 1862, Ambrose Burnside assumed full command of the Army of the Potomac. On Sunday January 25,1863, he was relieved of command.

Burnside tried, goodness knows he tried. He had been a close friend to General McClellan, but he recognized McClellan's errors. He was determined to avoid McClellan's mistakes. He knew President Lincoln had accused McClellan of *'having the slows'*. He knew President Lincoln had also thought McClellan reluctant to attack. So upon taking command, he immediately prepared a plan of action that called for quick aggressive action. The day Burnside finished the report, it was on its way to the president for his approval.

Burnside's plan called for the army to move to Fredericksburg, Virginia. Fredericksburg is approximately 60 miles north of Richmond. From there, he planned to move directly on Richmond. Lincoln warned Burnside that the destruction of Lee's army, not the capture of Richmond was his goal. However, he approved the plan, "provided the general moves quickly." Burnside did move quickly.

Two days after receiving Lincoln's approval, he put his army in motion.

There was a problem however. Fredericksburg lies on the south side of the Rappahannock River. Burnside and his men were on the north side. So Burnside ordered pontoon trains to be delivered so his engineers could build a bridge across the river. In keeping with the president's request, he wanted them delivered and the bridge built immediately.

Unfortunately, that sense of urgency did not accompany his order. Burnside forwarded his request for material to Halleck. Halleck handed the project off to an underling. Somewhere along the line, the idea of urgency was lost. The army camped on the edge of the river for eight days, waiting for their bridge.

When Burnside first arrived in Fredericksburg, he reported that "the enemy does not seem to be in force." That situation quickly changed as Burnside waited for his bridges. Lee brought forces into Fredericksburg during the delay and by the time the first pontoon arrived, Lee had placed General Longstreet's regiments all along a ridge called Marye's Heights. Marye's Heights looked right down into Fredericksburg and right down on Burnside's troops.

Burnside's plan, which might have succeeded had it been executed as designed, now seemed unworkable. The Rebels had taken the high ground and were firmly entrenched. An attack on that position seemed disastrous. President Lincoln even drew up an alternative plan, a plan which would not have included attacking Marye's Heights. However Generals Halleck and Burnside convinced the president that they did not have enough time to put his plan into place. Reluctantly, he agreed to let Burnside use his best judgement.

In the end, the pontoons arrived and a bridge was built, but by this time, General Lee's position was even more formidable. Lee had extended the line he'd started at Marye's Heights all along a seven-mile crest. That crest overlooked the river, the city, and Union troops. One artillery commander promised General Longstreet that "a chicken could not live on that field when we open on it." General Longstreet himself told General Lee, "General, if you put every man on the other side of the Potomac on that field to approach me over the same line, and give me plenty of ammunition, I will kill them all before they reach my line."

Burnside studied the Rebel troops on the south side of the river. He understood they commanded the heights, but once again McClellan's repeated failures came to mind. Burnside decided to keep with his pledge to be aggressive. He decided to continue with his plan. "Gentlemen," he announced to his subordinates, "the first step is to build that pontoon bridge."

Strangely, the Rebels didn't offer much resistance to this move. Shots were exchanged and some Rebel sharpshooters picked on the engineers, but they made no real move to contest the movement. Perhaps Burnside should have taken this as a omen?

He did not, and the result was the Battle of Fredericksburg. As General Lee watched the Union troops attack, attack, and attack the entrenched Confederates, he said, "It is well that war is so terrible. We should grow too fond of it." Days later a man who observed the battle described it to President Lincoln. It was *"butchery"* he told the president. He was correct. 12,600 casualties for the North, 4,200 for the South.

General Lee wrote his daughter that "General Burnside and his army will not eat their promised Christmas dinner in Richmond today."

Lincoln came to the conclusion that General Burnside had given his best, but perhaps Burnside himself had been correct; perhaps his best was not enough. Perhaps the job was too much for him.

Sadly, President Lincoln had to admit, he had still not found his commanding general.

"So what does this defeat mean then?" mumbled Jacob around a mouthful of lunch. He and Thomas had taken a lunch break at a nearby tavern. They sat by the fireplace hoping to ward off the day's chill.

Thomas' face scrunched in displeasure. "Don't talk with your mouth full! Goodness, Jacob, as if you didn't know better."

Jacob gave a small eye roll but swallowed before continuing with his question. He washed his bite down with a drink and then said, "So where do we go from here? What's next for the army?"

Thomas shifted some food around on his plate as he formed his answer. "We'll go into winter camp; the President will select a new commander and the war will continue in the spring." Thomas put his fork down. "Goodness, I never expected this rebellion to go on this long." He thought back to the days when Virginia was discussing secession. That seemed like a lifetime ago. So much had happened since then, both to the country and to the two lunch companions. "Let me ask you, Jacob. As you look back, how do you think we're doing now?"

Jacob paused the loaded fork that was headed toward his mouth. "How we're doing? You mean how's the Army of the Potomac doing?"

Thomas shook his head. "No, actually, I want to know how you are doing and what you think of your current situation. It's been a while now since we agreed to join President Lincoln's staff, and I wanted to know what you think. In other words," Thomas continued, "I suppose, I'm asking 'How's life?'"

Jacob was a bit surprised by the question, but he had been expecting something of the sort. He knew Thomas had been giving his own situation a great deal of thought since his father's visit. And Jacob had been giving his situation a great deal of thought, too. To be honest, Dr. Henderson's visit had caused Jacob a great deal of pain. Not the doctor himself of course; he had been nothing but wonderful. But seeing Thomas spend time with his father, reminded Jacob how much he had lost. There wasn't a day that he did not miss his father, his mother and his sister. He missed Salem, its rolling hills, and beautiful forests. He missed the farms and the streams. He missed the beauty of Southern

Indiana. After all, it was the only home he had ever known. He grieved and ached at his loss.

Jacob was also intelligent enough to appreciate the great place in which he had happened to stumble. Had you told him that an 11 year old orphan would run away without a lick of anything to his name and would end up working in the White House, why he never would have believed it for a second! What an accident of fate! He had had absolutely no idea where or how he would live when he stepped off that train back in 1861. He'd only wanted to escape. Now he worked at the White House.

He also knew no one waited for him back in Indiana. Indiana had been wonderful but that life was finished. Washington, D.C. was home now. Jacob placed his fork on his plate and looked Thomas in the eye. "Mr. Henderson, I cannot thank you enough for all you have done for me. I do not know what would have happened had we not chanced to meet. I'm staying with what I told your father. Life is perfect."

Thomas ducked his head and then answered, "I'd like to thank you, Jacob. You've made my life better." He thrust his hand toward Jacob, offering a handshake. "I would be very pleased if you would agree to continue the relationship. I don't know what comes next, but based on the past, I think we can say that it will be interesting!"

Jacob happily took the offered hand and shook. "To interesting times!"

And the times were interesting indeed. January 01, 1863 dawned, brightly and crisply. It was the day that Mr. Lincoln had set as his deadline. He had promised he would sign the Proclamation on New Year's Day if the South did not end their rebellion. To Mr. Lincoln's disappointment, but not surprise, the South had not ended the rebellion.

Nevertheless, many people were sure Mr. Lincoln would not sign the document. After all, there had been much hue and cry from many people. Surely Mr. Lincoln would not ignore their opinions.

There had been that terrible loss at Fredericksburg. Surely Mr. Lincoln would not sign it after that disaster!

Some people were sure that if the president signed it, mass desertions would occur. These folks were sure that the vast majority of soldiers would be against the idea of emancipation. Some were, but many more of the soldiers favored signing, not out of a concern for enslaved people necessarily but because they had come to believe it would shorten the war.

People warned that congressmen were against it. A bill was introduced after all, a resolution branding emancipation "a high crime against the Constitution". That resolution was voted down handily. Instead Congress passed the Enabling Act, requiring slavery be abolished in West Virginia before it could be admitted as the 35th state.

When Thursday, January 01,1863 dawned, there was uncertainty. What would the president do?

The day started as all New Year's Days had started during the Lincoln administration. The doors of the White House were swung wide open to the public. Access was granted to anyone who wished to come in. Diplomats, dignitaries, and private citizens, all mingled together.

At 9:00 a.m. the doors were opened, and waves of people flooded the White House. Mr. Lincoln shook hands with hundreds of people. He shook hands for hours. One observer said "the president's hand and arm were moving like a pump handle."

Another onlooker commented, "The president looked like he was sawing wood."

But at 2:00 p.m. Mr. Lincoln eased away from the crowd. He made his way to his second-story office where a large document sat on the table. Mr. Lincoln read it carefully. He had found an error in an earlier copy and had ordered a correction. Satisfied with this copy, he reached out to select a steel pen. He dipped the pen in ink; but then he paused.

He paused, not out of trepidation, but rather because his hand was trembling. He looked at it and announced, "I have shaken so many hands, it feels paralyzed!" Mr. Lincoln was not pausing because of second thoughts. He knew his signature would be examined for years, and he did not want people to look at a weak signature and feel he hesitated. There was no hesitation. No, Mr. Lincoln was sure. He told the assembled group, "I have never in my life felt more certain that I was doing right, than I do in signing this paper. My whole soul is in it." He gave his hand a chance to rest, and then he proudly affixed his signature to the document. When done, he examined it, gave a small laugh and said, "That will do!"

Satisfied with the issuance of the Emancipation Proclamation, he turned his attention back to his other problem, who should replace Burnside? Who should lead the Army of the Potomac? After weighing his options, he decided on an experienced veteran of the Eastern War, General Joseph Hooker.

Mr. Lincoln offered command to General Hooker. He quickly accepted.

On Monday, January 26, 1863, Major General Joseph Hooker took command of the Army of the Potomac. The appointment was strongly supported by the country.

Lincoln's first constituency, the army, applauded the movement. Hooker was one of theirs. He had been with them since the beginning. He had fought in the Peninsula Campaign. That's when Thomas had met General Hooker. General Kearny had introduced them. Kearny and Hooker had fought side by side at the Battle of Williamsburg. The two were much alike.

Like Kearny, Hooker had criticized McClellan for his lack of aggressiveness during the campaign. He openly criticized his failure to capture Richmond. Speaking about his commander, Hooker said, "He is not only not a soldier, but he does not know what soldiership is."

At the Battle of Antietam Hooker fought against Stonewall Jackson's men. He'd cut a strong figure in the saddle, riding his horse Colonel up and down the battlefield, urging his men on. Then he'd been wounded. He'd recovered in time to lead brutal frontal assaults against the Rebels at Fredericksburg.

Hooker was an opinionated man. He had no problem sharing his opinions with the world. After Fredericksburg, Hooker was quoted by a *New York Times* army correspondent as saying that, "Nothing would go right until we had a dictator, and the sooner the better."

Lincoln knew all this including the quote about the dictator, but he appreciated Hooker's fighting spirit and style and decided he was the man for the job. Lincoln wrote a letter to the newly-appointed general part of which stated, "I have heard, in such way as to believe it, of you recently saying that both the army and the government needed a dictator. Of course it was not for this, but in spite of it, that I have given you the command. Only those generals who gain success can set up dictators. What I now ask of you is military success, and I will risk the dictatorship."

Hooker went to work immediately. He first issued orders that would improve his soldiers lives. Supplies were brought in by the wagonload, food was improved and furloughs were granted. The soldiers wholeheartedly approved and saluted their new commander.

Lincoln came to visit the army and he could clearly see the improvement. Morale had plummeted after Fredericksburg. Now at a review, the president saw an improved army. He saw thousands of marching men, bayonets glittering in the winter air. He saw thousands of horsemen, heard rolling drums, and saw the flags proudly waving.

During the visit Lincoln said to Hooker, "If you get to Richmond, General..." Hooker interrupted, 'Excuse me, Mr. President, there is no "if" in this case.'"

General Hooker continued, "I have the finest army on the planet, I have the finest army the sun ever shone on. ... if the enemy does not run, God help them. May God have mercy on General Lee, for I will have none."

Lincoln was impressed and he was hoping that General Hooker was correct. But Lincoln had also heard such words before. To be on the safe side, he decided to put another plan into play.

When Thomas got to work on Monday February 2, 1863, a note was perched on his chair. It was in the president's handwriting. "Thomas, I would appreciate it if you would attend a meeting in my office today at 2:00 p.m. A. Lincoln."

Later that day, Thomas turned the corner toward the second-floor office to see Charles Dana coming down the hallway. "Two o'clock meeting?" Mr. Dana asked with a smile.

"Yes, sir."

"Then shall we?" He knocked on the frame of the open door, and the two entered the president's office.

Mr. Lincoln looked up at their knock. "Oh, yes, gentlemen, good, good. Come in. Sit." When the two had dropped into chairs, Mr. Lincoln came right to the point. "Gentlemen, last Friday, January 30, General Grant assumed immediate command of the entire expedition against the Mississippi river town, Vicksburg."

"Ahhhh," said Mr. Dana.

Thomas didn't say much of anything. He didn't know all that much about Mississippi or Vicksburg. He'd heard of both of them of course, but that was about it.

"Now I know Grant has been nosing around down there, but he's made no real progress on this front to date. Some people tell me he's stuck in the mud down there, and you see, that's the problem. I hear tell he is a bumbler I hear he is a butcher. I hear he drinks I hear he is insubordinate." Mr. Lincoln ticked the points off his fingers as he listed them. "But gentlemen, I know he fights: Fort Henry, Fort

Donaldson and Shiloh to name three. I've told his doubters straight out, I can't spare this man; he fights."

The president began to pace his office as he talked. "We have a saying in Illinois, 'where there's smoke, there's fire.' Now I full-well know that isn't always the case, but we sure seem to have a lot of smoke in the air concerning our General Grant. Now Charles, Thomas started me thinking on this. Thomas, would you please share the information about General Grant you placed in your last report?"

That request caught Thomas a bit unaware, but he summarized his speculation that Grant was a victim of politics and past reputation. Charles Dana did not speak, but he listened intently. He nodded as Thomas spoke. When Thomas had finished, Dana said, "You know I met Grant briefly last year…"

The president jumped like a cat on a mouse, "I do know that, and I do know the quality of your work." Then the president laid it on the table. "Would you be willing to go out to Mississippi and investigate Grant for me? Would you get to the bottom of this and find out what kind of a man, what kind of a commander he is? To put it another way, is there fire under that smoke?"

Mr. Dana blinked rapidly a few times but answered in a clear voice. "Of course sir," he paused. "but there is the question of what my purpose might be. Do you want me to show up with the announced purpose of evaluating the commanding general?"

"No, Mr. Dana, that won't do. You need to go out under another set of orders. I could order you to reinvestigate cotton speculators. We'll find something. Will you go?"

"At once, Mr. President." That night Dana wrote a letter to a friend. "I am here as a special commissioner of the War Department, a sort of official spectator and companion to the movements of this part of the campaign, charged particularly with overseeing and regulating the paymasters, and generally with making myself useful." Of course his real job was to tell Mr. Lincoln what kind of a general he had in Ulysses S. Grant. Two days later, Charles Dana was heading west toward the Army of the Tennessee and its commander.

Two days after that, Thomas came to work to find another note on his chair. "Thomas, would you and Jacob please step upstairs and see me? A Lincoln."

Once again, the door was open and the quick knock earned them admittance. "Ah, yes, my intrepid young assistants. Well, at least I hope you are intrepid." Mr. Lincoln smiled broadly as he spoke. He reached out and put an arm around Jacob. He began walking the youngster toward the southern facing windows. "Now Jacob, a few days back we had the chance to whittle a bit and chat."

"Yes sir!' Jacob quickly responded.

Mr. Lincoln stopped in front of the window. It looked out on the southern lawn of the White House. The walls next to the window had green wallpaper but it was hard to see since most of the wallpaper was covered with maps. Mr. Lincoln turned to one specific map. It was of the western section of the war. "I asked you a question then, and I want to repeat it today." He reached up and tapped a spot on the map. "Do you wish to see Indiana again?" He looked down at the young man.

Jacob stammered a bit, but he got it out. "Oh yes sir, Mr. President."

"Good man, Jacob," he tousled Jacob's hair.

Mr. Lincoln turned to Thomas. "Thomas, I have need of your talents. I have a special assignment, and I need a trusted confidant to carry it out. Are you willing?"

"Of course sir, how may I serve?"

Mr. Lincoln said, "I need you and Jacob, if you're willing, to make your way to the Great State of Indiana. I need some assistance there. If you're willing, Mr. Hay and Mr. Nicolay will explain the situation and give you your marching orders." Thomas instantly replied, "Of course, Mr. President."

Jacob beamed as he looked up at his president. "Of course, Mr. President. However we can serve."

That's how Jacob and Thomas found themselves preparing for an assignment in Indiana.

Chapter 10

"Mr. Lincoln gave a lot of thought to making this trip himself," Nicolay told Thomas and Jacob. "Then things got too hectic for him to leave the White House, but that tells you how important this endeavor is to the president."

Thomas, Jacob, and John Hay were all gathered in Nicolay's office. John Hay was standing next to Nicolay's desk. He looked at the desk for a second and then slid a stack of papers over a foot or so. Having created a nice little space, he then preceded to perch on the edge of the desk. Nicolay gave him a disapproving look.

"Jacob," Hay said, pretending not to notice Nicolay, "We're having some trouble back in our beloved home state. A bit of antiwar sentiment."

Jacob gave him a very puzzled look, "But I don't understand; Indiana is in the Union. We support the president, and we support the war."

"Well, you've hit it there, Jacob," Nicolay said, "Some people in Indiana support the president and the war, but some don't, and their actions are presenting us with a problem."

Jacob huffed, "I know they don't, but I still think everyone in the North should support the war!" he asserted indignantly.

"Oh, we would all agree with that, Jacob!"

"If only," echoed Nicolay.

"But" John Hay said, "remember when we talked about those 1860 election results? Some of the people who voted against Mr. Lincoln are now actively working against his war efforts. And Indiana is only one example. We've got similar problems in Ohio and Illinois."

"And right here in the capital!" Nicolay said. "Did you hear the speech that Congressman Vallandigham of Ohio gave recently?"

Thomas and Jacob both shook their heads "no".

"Well I am paraphrasing here…" he looked at the ceiling and began speaking, "As I recall, the good congressman accused the president of spending money without limit, a million dollars a day, pouring blood like water, referring to Fredericksburg, and he said that the only trophies from this war would be defeat, debt, taxation, and death. He concluded by advising his listeners to 'throw King Lincoln from his throne.' When he finished, members of the House gave him a standing ovation. Now that is definitely not the response we wanted from the House of Representatives. As you can see gentlemen, we have problems."

Nicolay continued, "Right now, Indiana is the linchpin, so we're going to deal with that situation first."

Thomas jumped in, "What exactly is the situation?"

John Hay bowed his head at Nicolay and said, "Professor?"

Nicolay returned the bow. "As you wish. Well, Indiana is very important to us. Indiana has been very kind and supportive. When President Lincoln issued a nationwide call for 75,000 volunteers in 1861, Indiana pledged to provide 10,000 of those volunteers all by herself."

"Our great state did more than promise," Hay interjected. "We delivered! Within a week 12,000 Hoosiers had signed up for service!"

"Ah, yes," said Nicolay continuing. "Indiana's Governor Oliver Morton has indeed been a staunch ally. He has provided our cause with men, money and weapons. That's wonderful and we all most certainly appreciate it, but as we all know only too well, the war has lasted far longer than we first thought - or hoped. As the war has continued, Governor Morton's support has not flinched, but the support of other Hoosiers...well..."

John Hay jumped back in, "Just as all Hoosiers did not vote for President Lincoln, all did not vote for Governor Morton. In fact, sadly, after the recent election, the Democrats now control the legislature. Morton still sits as governor but he is threatened. The Democrats introduced bills criticizing both Governor Morton and President Lincoln. They have accused Governor Morton of acting like a tyrant or a dictator instead of a governor. They are sure he is exceeding his authority."

"My," Nicolay innocently asked, "who else has been accused of that I wonder?"

"Hmmmph!" Hay responded. "We, on the other hand think Governor Morton has earned the lifelong gratitude of Union soldiers."

Nicolay continued, "They called for investigations of what they call 'Republican abuses of power and the infringement of civil liberties.' They are also threatening to cut off all state funding for the war."

"And it's not just the legislators," Hay added, "In Morgan County, just south of Indianapolis, our soldiers found some deserters and tried to arrest them. Citizens took up arms against the soldiers, and we had to send in cavalry to restore calm."

Jacob was aghast. "Indiana citizens took up arms against Union soldiers? Cavalry had to be called to control Indiana citizens?"

"Sad to say, Jacob," Hay replied. "It's true."

Nicolay continued, "Things are becoming more intense. After the Emancipation Proclamation, many citizens became less supportive of our efforts. After all, many Indiana citizens originally came from Kentucky, Virginia, and North Carolina, slave states all. In the beginning when preserving the Union was the cry, they were supportive. Now that emancipation has been placed on the table, some of these citizens find their support wavering."

"So all of this is to say, Governor Morton is becoming a bit, well…what word am I searching for Nicolay?"

"Nervous?"

"Good choice! Nervous, unsettled, perhaps even rattled. We need a strong message to go out that assures him we have both supported and appreciated him; we do support him now, and we will continue to support him!"

"He also needs to hear that we are very aware of his situation."

"Exactly!"

Thomas was still a bit unclear, "And a letter from the president won't serve?"

"No, Thomas, we think a more robust response is needed. The president will, of course, write the letter, but we think the situation requires more. We feel it is important that Mr. Lincoln's assurances be hand delivered to the governor along with a strong verbal assurance."

"From a trusted White House aide!" Nicolay inserted.

"From a trusted White house aide," Hay agreed. "We need to make sure Governor Morton knows that we appreciate all his fine work. We need to make certain he knows that he is not alone or forgotten! And we think you, and Jacob of course, are the perfect messengers."

Thomas must have had a worried look on his face.

"Don't worry, we'll create the talking points for you, but it really is vitally important that you personally assure the governor that we are with him. As we said, this is not just happening in Indiana. Similar things are occurring in Illinois and Ohio."

"We must have the support of these crucial western states. Should they turn away from us, the situation would be dire indeed!"

"In all honesty, the war could hang in the balance."

At this comment, Thomas jumped in, "Gentlemen! No! You said it yourselves! The very war may be hanging in the balance! You need a trusted White House aide. I am a lowly assistant secretary. Why are we having this conversation? I am merely Thomas Henderson."

Startled, Hay and Nicolay looked at Thomas in disbelief.

Nicolay recovered first, "Oh, Thomas, have we been so remiss?"

Hay jumped in, "Thomas, we know what we said. We know the requirements. We know who we are talking to."

"Most importantly," Nicolay said, "Mr. Lincoln knows who we are talking to."

"Yes!" Hay agreed pointing his finger toward Jacob and then Thomas, "We are talking to both of you."

At this, Jacob spoke up, "I feel woefully underprepared, and I wonder about your reasoning, but I'm willing to do what's asked if you figure I'm the fella for the job!"

A feeling of unhappiness and intense uncertainty swept over Thomas. This task was too important; he was too minor a player. He did not have the experience. After a minute of thinking, he responded. "Well, I also am woefully underprepared and I also wonder about your reasoning. No, gentleman," Thomas shook his head and began rising from his chair. "I am not the man for this job. You need to find someone more experienced, I am sure! Thank you for your consideration and your kind words, but I am not prepared for this mission. This is far too large a job to place on my small plate." And with that, he stood, nodded at each man and left the office.

Jacob jumped up and was right on his heels. "But Mr. Henderson, we were asked to help!" His tone expressed his surprise and dismay at Henderson's actions. "We told the president we'd help."

But Thomas would hear none of it. "They made a mistake when they asked us. We are not prepared; we are not ready. It would be a grave mistake to go. I fear we would do more harm than good. No, Jacob, they must find someone else. Don't worry; they'll soon realize that. Someone else will be in that saddle soon enough."

Thomas was back in his cranny bent over his work. Jacob was…well Thomas wasn't exactly sure where Jacob was. He had been noticeably absent ever since the contentious meeting. "*I suppose he's showing his displeasure,*" Thomas thought. "*Well too bad. I'm right! Of course he wants to go; he's from Indiana. But if the message is that important, and I'm sure it is, I am certainly not the one to deliver such a…*"

Suddenly, Thomas felt a presence loom up behind him. In an instant, the figure was right over his shoulder. Before he could even turn he heard, (and felt) President Lincoln. "THOMAS!" Mr. Lincoln practically spat the word out. Thomas jumped. Thomas had never heard the president use a tone like this, well, at least Mr. Lincoln had never used that tone with him. An immediate surge of panic raced through Thomas. Icy fingers of fear began gripping his intestines. He felt his stomach flip over and over. He hadn't felt like this since his father had found out he was skipping school and carousing around New York City.

"Did I hear this correctly?" the president continued in the same menacing tone. "Did I hear you

say I was *wrong?* Did I hear you say you wouldn't
GO?" The last word fairly crackled with anger.

Thomas spun around to face the president but
no words came out. Somehow his mouth had become
filled with sand.

Mr. Lincoln looked Thomas square in the eye.
"You are qualified to go to Indiana because I *say* you
are qualified to go!" He paused for a long second, his
eyes boring into Thomas, "And I say you are qualified
because you are!" His tone softened a bit. "Thomas, I
know your mettle. I know your experience. Let me
ask you, are you not the man who left college and
spent a year studying the Army of the Potomac? Are
you not the man who wrote a very detailed and finely
reasoned analysis of General McClellan? Are you not
the man General Kearny trusted?"

Mr. Lincoln's tone softened even more. "Ah,
Thomas, like most people, you lack the eye to see
yourself as others do. I sense your trepidation but I
assure you, you have what it takes. I would not ask
you otherwise, you must believe me."

"You must see this mission is very important to
me, it's important to the war effort, I believe it's
important to the country. I knew what I was doing
when I selected you. Perhaps I should have spent a bit
of time with you explaining my reasoning, but I was

sure you were my man. I am sure you are my man. You can see this mission to its successful conclusion, and I'm counting on you."

Listening to these words, Thomas felt one load lift and another one settle. He was relieved the president had such respect for his abilities, but he was also a bit disappointed in himself that he had displeased the man he held in such high esteem. He placed President Lincoln second only to his own father.

Thomas softly spoke, "Thank you, Mister President. Of course I will go."

"Good!" Mr. Lincoln laid a kindly hand on Thomas' shoulder. His tone had significantly softened. "I will lay out all the points I wish you to make to Governor Morton, but the most important one is this: make sure the good governor knows we stand firmly with him. Make sure he knows Indiana is important to us, and make sure he knows we will not leave him high and dry. Now Thomas, this is important as well. Governor Morton is a fine man and a firm friend. But he can get…well…a little skittish. Your job is to reassure him that we're with him all the way. Can you do that?"

"Sir, I will give it my all!" Thomas quickly responded.

"Then that will do." President Lincoln pressed on Thomas' shoulder and then turned to leave. He paused in the doorway, turning back to Thomas. "Oh, and please take Jacob to Salem while you're out there. I think he'd like that." He turned and took a half step more before pausing again to add, "But don't forget to bring him back!" He grinned at Thomas and left.

Thomas found that he had half risen from his chair. He flopped back down and began to settle himself from the encounter. As he did so, he was very surprised to find Jacob in the room. Evidently he had quietly joined them in the last few minutes.

"So we're going to Indiana then, sir?" Jacob asked.

Thomas shook his head as if he could still not quite believe it but he said, "We are indeed young man. You may begin to pack your bags."

While Jacob and Thomas were preparing for their Indiana sojourn, General Ulysses S Grant was in Tennessee pondering the state of his world. He didn't like what he saw. He could see the Mississippi River flowing by and that sight did not make him happy.

He had nothing against the river itself of course, but the Mississippi River rolled southward through the heart of the Confederacy. During the first two years of the war, the North had captured major sections of this crucial river. The North controlled New Orleans, Louisiana, in the south, and Cairo, Illinois, in the north. However, they lacked control of one vital stretch, the hundred and some-mile stretch between Vicksburg, Mississippi, and Port Hudson, Louisiana. As it happened, this vital stretch was crucial. The western Confederate states produced many important supplies that the eastern Confederate states heavily counted upon. Eastbound trains picked up these vital supplies at Vicksburg.

Vicksburg itself was built on a high bluff overlooking a horseshoe-shaped bend in the river. The Confederates had taken advantage of that bluff and fortified the city. Heavy guns were prominent, ready to repel any attack.

Many believed that this strip of land and river was crucially important. Whoever controlled it, controlled the outcome of the war. Abraham Lincoln called the city of Vicksburg, "the key to the war." His counterpart, Jefferson Davis said that Vicksburg was "the nailhead that holds the two halves of the Confederacy together."

President Lincoln wanted the military to capture that nailhead. He wanted to hold that key. He wanted the city of Vicksburg taken and the Mississippi River in Union hands. Of course, President Davis had a much different desire.

The Union's first effort to capture Mr. Lincoln's key was made by the Union Brown Water Navy. The North had created a fleet of ironclad boats. Nothing like these boats had ever been seen on the Mississippi. The Mississippi was often in a muddy brown state so these boats had been nicknamed the Brown Water Navy.

In June of 1862, the Brown Water Navy made its first attempt. Admiral David Farragut sailed a fleet upriver. Honestly, he expected to take Vicksburg easily. After all, Baton Rouge, Louisiana and Natchez, Mississippi had surrendered without a shot being fired. Once anchored below the city, he sent a message to the town fathers. His message demanded surrender and he waited for their response.

When it came, it shocked him. "Mississipians don't know and refuse to learn how to surrender." it read. If the Federal commanders thought they could teach the Vicksburg residents otherwise, "Let them come and try."

Foote did not have the men to conquer the city, and the geography, the heights specifically, meant that if he shelled the city, the shelling would have little effect. He could simply not point his cannon high enough to inflict damage on the city. Farragut was forced to discontinue his efforts.

After that, the decision was made to give General Grant the task of capturing Vicksburg. And why not Grant? Expectations were high. After all, Western troops had already earned victories at Fort Henry, Fort Donelson, and Shiloh. "Add one more victory to the list!" was the cry, and Grant intended to do that. In December of 1862, Grant launched a two-prong attack south from Tennessee toward Vicksburg. That attack; however, failed. The Confederates had been able to force the Yankees back north, northward away from Vicksburg.

Grant then spent the next two months trying to discover a successful strategy. He searched for the key to the puzzle that was Vicksburg. Nothing worked. "Grant's mired in the Mississippi mud," lamented President Lincoln.

Grant was worried. Grant wanted to be in charge but he realized he needed to achieve success to stay in charge. He had only to look at the list of Army of the Potomac generals to understand that: Scott, McDowell, McClellan, Pope and Burnside, none had realized success; all were gone from command.

To add to his problems, Grant knew he had plenty of political enemies, men who were jealous, men who wanted his job. They continually told Lincoln that Grant was a failure, a drunkard, a butcher.

Sometimes the attacks were right in his face, published for all to see. The *Indianapolis Journal* printed a front-page article labeling Grant a failure. The *Saint Louis Republican* condemned Grant both as a person and a military officer. Sometimes the attacks were made behind his back. Grant knew all this.

But Grant had immense faith in himself. He had learned much since he'd been given command. Every single battle had taught him something. Some had taught him a great deal. Shiloh, for instance, had greatly changed him.

Before the battle, Grant, like many others, believed a strong Union push would win the war. One Union victory would compel the South to surrender. Shiloh totally disabused him of that idea. He walked away from that battle completely convinced it was going to take everything the North had to force the South into submission. He knew now that he faced a strong determined foe and no one battle or push was going to defeat the Rebels. He knew now that it would take much more to make them give up. Now, Vicksburg and Port Hudson strengthened that conviction.

After much study and contemplation, Grant decided in late March that the best strategy would be to combine his forces with the Brown Water Navy.

It was also in late March that Charles Dana arrived. Grant knew Dana. They had met the year before. Though certainly not friends, the two had gotten along well.

Earlier, Grant had sent notice to the War Department that his men were not being paid on time. Dana announced that he had arrived to look into that issue. Grant listened politely, but he did not buy that story. Grant was sure he knew the real reason Dana was in his camp. He was sure Dana was Lincoln's spy.

Some of Grant's lieutenants wanted to turn him away. Grant had other ideas. "Let him see," he told his commanders, "Let him see what we can do."

Grant went back to work and Dana settled into camp. When Grant moved, Dana moved. Dana was treated with great respect and hospitality.

After a few weeks, Secretary of War Stanton asked Dana for his initial report. Dana replied that he found Grant to be "modest, honest, and judicial. . . . not an original or brilliant man, but sincere, thoughtful, deep, and gifted with a courage that never faltered. Although quiet and hard to know, he loved a humorous story and the company of his friends." His initial impression was that Grant was indeed the man for the job.

He continued to stay with Grant's army. The more he saw, the more he appreciated the character of the man. Charles Dana was becoming one of Ulysses S. Grant's most firm supporters. Every one of his dispatches back east made the point that 'Grant is the man.' However, it would take action by Grant to convince the White House that Dana was correct.

Chapter 11

Thomas and Jacob were huddled together, shoulder to shoulder over a table at the War Department. A map of the United States was spread before them.

"From here," Thomas said dropping the forefinger of his left hand emphatically on Washington City, "to there!" He placed a equally emphatic right-handed forefinger on Salem, Indiana.

Completely surprised, Jacob spun to face Thomas, "We're going to Salem?"

"Well, yes," Thomas said with satisfaction. "Mr. Lincoln thought it was a good idea." He'd kept that destination a secret and now he was very glad he had. The look on Jacob's face was well worth the wait.

Jacob let out a deep breath. "Well, now I'll be!" he said in a very satisfied voice. "So that is what he meant."

"I'm sorry?" asked Thomas not understanding his meaning.

"No, nothing sir, just putting parts of a puzzle together." Jacob happily rubbed his hands together, feeling both anticipation and satisfaction.

Thomas nodded; he was pleased Jacob seemed excited by the news. Now, however, the question was exactly how was he going to get Jacob to Salem, Indiana? Getting from the White House to say, Alexandria was one thing. Getting from the White House to Salem, Indiana, was quite another. Especially considering they would be moving across a country embroiled in war. It was true that the vast majority of the fighting was south of their route, but Thomas had come to believe in the adage 'You never know.' Antietam had occurred after all and that was in the North. Well, fine it was in Maryland, and Maryland was a border state, but the point was made. Maryland was north of the previous fighting. Was there a chance that the Rebels would launch another northward thrust? Might they invade the West this time, say try to take Cincinnati? Thomas didn't think so, but he hadn't thought Jeb Stuart would ride around the Union army yet again either.

Still, Mr. Lincoln had asked them to go west, so west they would go. That meant decisions had to be made. What was the easiest route? What was the cheapest route? Where should they stay? Where would they sleep? He was determined to go, but he was also worried. This trip would be expensive. How was he going to pay for all this?

His reverie was broken by John Hay's bright tone. "So this is where you are hiding!" said John Hay as he walked into the room. "Planning the western adventure? Good, very good. I'm right on time then." He walked up to the table, glanced at the map and patted both Thomas and Jacob on the shoulder in a rather fatherly fashion.

"Before you get too deeply into the matter, I've come to make your lives a little easier." He pulled a packet from his inside pocket and began handing papers to Thomas.

"First of all, here is your route. Well, it's yours if you approve it. Thank the War Department for that. Secondly, here is your itinerary for that route. The complete package from start to finish. And lastly, and of course, your U.S. Government travel vouchers."

He looked at Thomas' face and laughed, "You didn't think we were sticking you with the cost of this trip did you? Never good sir! "

Thomas didn't respond but he didn't have to. His relief was obvious.

"Now, let's see what's here." Hay returned to the task of pulling papers from the packet. "First class tickets for the trains, upper-deck tickets for your steamer trip." He caught Thomas' look of surprise.

"Yes, first class. Mr. Lincoln very much appreciates you making this trip."

At the mention of upper-deck tickets, Jacob jumped in. "What steamer trip?" Jacob had made the trip from Indiana to Washington City once before and it had not involved a steamboat.

"The steamer trip," John Hay answered, "from Pittsburgh, Pennsylvania, to Louisville, Kentucky." He placed his finger on the map and traced the Ohio River from Pittsburgh southwest to Louisville. "Trains from here to Pittsburgh, steamboat on down to Louisville."

"Never been on a river steamer before," mused Jacob.

"No," Thomas agreed, "but you did make the voyage from Norfolk to the capital last July."

"True," Jacob admitted slowly. He extended the word as he spoke, agreeing that he had made that journey but showing he wasn't sure about another such river journey.

John Hay promised, "This boat will be even larger than that boat. Those steamboats are the queens of the rivers. You'll love it!" he promised. Then he paused a minute, "Then from Louisville to Salem!" He looked at Jacob. "I envy you, you know? It's been a long time since I've seen Salem."

Jacob nodded and solemnly said, "I'll pay special attention and bring back plenty of memories. I promise to share them all with you."

"That will do, Jacob, that will do."

The trio spent a few more minutes going over details and then Hay left to head back to the White House.

Almost as soon as he did, a War Department clerk slid over to Jacob's side. "Woo-eee!" he said shaking his head. "Steamboat? No way you'd get me on one of them! A soul's gotta be plum crazy to get on board one." He knitted his brow as he stared at Jacob, "Are you seriously thinking about getting on one of them death traps?"

"Well," Jacob said slowly, "some folks say they be safe enough."

The clerk gave him a disbelieving look. "No, listen here now! You're from Indiana ain't ya?" Jacob nodded and the clerk plunged on. "Then I'm sure you've heard of the *Lucy Walker* and what happened to her! I mean everybody has. Steamboats? Never!" He turned to walk back to his work. "Never!" he said again. The words trailed over his shoulder.

A Union private stood guard at the door. Of course he wasn't supposed to be listening, and of course he was. He peered at Jacob. "You ain't never heard of the *Lucy Walker*?" He shook his head in a disbelief. He peered more closely, "You sure you be from Indiana?"

"Ahh, get away with you! What would the likes of you be knowing about anything?" Jacob asked, waving the private away. "Get back to your important job of guarding that empty door!" Jacob gave him a hard look, "I mean unless that job is too much for you!" At that, the guard reddened, straightened up, and stared ahead into empty space.

Thomas was immersed in the documents and had missed the interaction. He finally placed the last paper back in the packet and started rolling up the map. Jacob returned the map to its drawer. "Thank you, Lieutenant," Thomas said, "you've been most helpful. We'll be returning to the White House now."

Jacob thought hard as they walked the few blocks. *"It had to be safe right? People have been journeying on them for years. And if Mr. Hay and Mr. Henderson both were on board...oh on board. Perhaps the not best turn of a phrase. Anyway if they both said it was safe..."*

Once back in the White House, Jacob set about to do a little digging. He found a reference to a book, *Steamboat Directory and Disasters on the Western Waters*, James T. Lloyd & Co, Cincinnati, Ohio. Jacob figured these folks would know about disasters. He immediately left for the Library of Congress. The librarian brought him a copy of the book and he soon found that the *Lucy Walker* was a steamboat that had been destroyed in an explosion. It happened on the Ohio River, right near Louisville in New Albany, Indiana. Evidently, the steamer's three boilers exploded almost simultaneously and the ship sank in a matter of minutes. Many lives were lost. It was indeed a disaster.

As he turned the pages things seemed to get worse. It appeared that the *Lucy Walker* was only one of a number of similar disasters, but then Jacob focused in on the date of the *Lucy Walker* disaster, 1844. 1844? *Heck, he hadn't even been born yet! The world was a much different place now,* he assured himself. That made him feel better. "Sure we're going to be just fine." he said aloud.

As he returned the book and walked back to work, however, he had to admit, he could not completely shake the memory of the *Lucy Walker.*

That memory did fade as the departure date came closer. There was so much to do. Jacob had made the trip from Indiana to Washington, D.C. in 1861 carrying his belongings in a cloth sack; a sack so light that he swung it over his shoulder, and stuck it under his railway seat. Now there were bags, satchels, trunks, and who knew what all? This was going to be a much different journey!

And it was hard to say who was more eager or perhaps the most nervous? Thomas had never been west before, never seen mountains like the Appalachians. This would be the longest trip Thomas had ever attempted. It was even longer than his first major trip, New York City to the College of William and Mary. Thomas was excited, and truth be told, a bit nervous.

Jacob was excited, well, because he was going home. Or was it home? He'd been struggling with this question for the last month and still had no real clear answer. He'd grown up in Indiana and despite the horrible tragedy of his family's deaths, he still had a decade or so of wonderful memories. It had been a good place to grow up, but the nation's capital was his home now, and he realized he was very happy with his new world. Of course he missed his family, but there was nothing he could do about that tragedy. The nation's capital was his new home and given everything, he could not have been more pleased. Like Thomas though, he was still nervous.

His nervousness came from a couple of sources. Would going back reopen wounds he had been working hard to cure? He had freely told Thomas that he would not change places if he were given the choice, but what would going back be like now, after all this change?

Jacob also had this fear that the first minute he showed up in Salem, the parson, who believed Jacob was in upstate New York with his Aunt Hezbayla, would grab him by the scruff of the neck and force him onto a New York bound train. Of course Jacob knew Thomas would not let this happen. What was the word Thomas had used? Oh, yes, irrational. He'd called it an irrational fear. Irrational or not, Jacob wasn't sure he wanted to see that parson.

Soon enough, the day of departure arrived. Once again Thomas and Jacob made their way through the early morning mist to the Baltimore and Ohio Depot. They boarded the train and were escorted to their first-class accommodations. First class all the way, D.C. to Baltimore to Pittsburgh! It didn't take them very long to get into the foothills of the Appalachians. Thomas was ecstatic. Foothills gave way to hills. Hills gave way to mountains. They were beautiful, Thomas decided. Magnificent.

Jacob pretended indifference, after all he'd crossed these mountains before. But the reality was, during his first crossing, he'd concentrated on plotting his escape and had not spent a single minute appreciating the landscape. This time he too would move from window to window, "oohing" and "aahing" over the beautiful sights.

Jacob truly appreciated the first-class accommodations. Thomas had only been on shorter train rides where the upgrade may not have been so important. Jacob on the other hand remembered being jammed up shoulder and elbow with his fellow passengers, day and night. He remembered the hard seats, the constant noise, the smoke from the engine, the less than pleasant smells and of course the terrible food.

Jacob declared first-class food to be "tremendous." Thomas did not share his enthusiasm but Thomas didn't know what the alternative was. Jacob did, and he assured him that this food was just fine. The way Jacob looked at it, they had a fair amount of pretty decent food. They each had a bunk and a bit of privacy. They were not jammed shoulder to elbow at all. As far as he was concerned, this was a fine journey, yes sir. If only those occasional flashes of the *Lucy Walker* disaster would stop popping up.

They arrived in Pittsburgh without incident.

Considering all that was involved, it turned out to be a relatively easy transfer from the railcar to the steamboat. The luggage was successfully loaded on a wagon and taken to the steamboat berth. They were stunned to see so many steamboats! Smoke rising from each smokestack as the steamboats sat tied up in a long row. Who knew they called Pittsburgh "Steamship City"? After a few false starts, the waggoneer found their steamship, the *Samuel A. Adams*.

Although he had never been on a steamboat before, Jacob instantly saw the advantages of upper-deck tickets. On his way to the upper deck, Jacob walked past wall-to-wall cotton bales, large wooden crates stacked floor to ceiling, livestock wandering in basically what amounted to temporary corrals, and tons of other types of freight. Jacob later learned that steamboat companies made a lot more money hauling freight than they did hauling passengers. If you didn't have an upper-deck ticket, you made your bed as best you could among all that freight. You also rode next to the red-hot boilers and brought your own food. Jacob could see that the lower deck was going to quickly get very crowded, sweaty, smelly, and dirty. "Well," Thomas said philosophically, "I would not enjoy the passage, but it will get them out west."

Life on the upper decks was a little bit different. "A little bit?" Jacob snorted, "It's a totally different world!" Jacob was right about that. The upper-deck passengers might pay double the rate of the lower decks, but if you could afford the extra, you received the extra. The upper-deck passengers had private rooms with beds. They ate in dining rooms and were served food that would challenge Washington, D.C.'s finest cuisine. Jacob and Thomas looked in on rooms that held gambling tables and bars and grills. The two different levels might have been two different universes. Thomas and Jacob thanked their lucky stars that they were living in the upper-deck universe for the next week or so.

Still Thomas quickly reminded Jacob, "Despite the elegant surroundings, we are not carefree!" Both Nicolay and Hay had taken Thomas aside to educate him on the dangers of the river, and he had shared those warnings with Jacob.

"I have been repeatedly warned that theft is a huge danger on these trips, lower and upper decks! Pickpockets and other thieves abound!' Thomas had repeatedly told Jacob. As he reissued his warning, Thomas patted his pockets to make sure his valuables were secure.

Jacob gave the dining room a hard gaze. He didn't see any obvious suspects, but that didn't mean they weren't there! Jacob's task was made a bit harder because, well, to be truthful Jacob wasn't exactly sure what he was looking for. What did a riverboat thief look like anyway? Nevertheless, he promised Thomas, "You can count on me sir. I'll keep a cold eye on 'em." Thomas smiled to himself but said nothing. After all, every little bit helped.

As they were surprised by the beautiful landscape on the train, they were enthralled by the beauty of the Ohio River Valley. They steamed along at a magnificent five miles per hour. As they shifted their gaze from one side to the other, they saw the farms nestled along the river banks, the forests that came to the rivers edge, and the numerous rivers and streams that poured into the Ohio. They saw the small towns spreading on the sides of the river. Occasionally, a larger town appeared. The captain sounded the whistle as they passed.

Jacobs saw eagles flying overhead and shared the tall tales the deckhands told him about the size of the fish right below their feet. The river got a bit wider each day. Both Thomas and Jacob had been impressed by the size of the river in Pittsburgh. "Oh, this is nothing!" a deckhand told Jacob. "When we get to Louisville, this here river's going to be almost a mile wide!" When Jacob shared this news with Thomas, Thomas didn't say anything, but he was quite sure that either Jacob or the deckhand were grossly exaggerating. *"A mile wide"* Thomas thought, and a smile spread over his face. *"I don't think so!"*

Southwest they sailed. Soon they were out of Pennsylvania and entering Ohio. Past Steubenville, past Marietta, and Portsmouth. Then came the Queen City, Cincinnati. Next they were sailing past Indiana towns and farms. Getting near now!

They passed the town of Madison, Indiana, and almost immediately came to the small town of Hanover, Indiana. There they were told the river makes an almost perfect "S"curve! One of the deckhands pointed to a bluff and told them there was a small college up there where a person could look down on the whole scene. Thomas smiled to himself again. *"Goodness colleges in Indiana!"* But then after all, Indiana had been a state for well over 40 years. *"Of course Indiana has colleges."* he chided himself, but he continued to smile none-the-less.

Madison was only some fifty miles northeast of Louisville, which meant the end of this journey was in sight. When the *Samuel A. Adams* bumped into the dock in Louisville the next day, they'd been sailing on the Ohio River one short week!

"Kentucky," Jacob thought as they debarked, *"is weird. Okay, not weird"* he quickly amended. Thomas

had told him that weird was a 'term of derision.' Kentucky was strange then, or perhaps a better word was different?

When the war broke out and people were choosing sides, Kentucky had chosen to join neither side. Kentucky had declared its neutrality. They joined Maryland, Delaware and Missouri in declaring neutrality. These so called border states said they were staying out of this struggle, yet they all ended up playing a role.

Kentucky was of immense importance during the war. Both sides coveted the state. In a letter to Senator O. H. Browning, Abraham Lincoln said, "I think to lose Kentucky is nearly the same as to lose the whole game. Kentucky gone, we cannot hold Missouri, nor, as I think, Maryland. These all against us, and the job on our hands is too large for us." The president valued Kentucky and strongly felt he must keep it in the Union.

It was rumored that Lincoln also said, "I hope to have God on my side, but I must have Kentucky!" Thomas did not know if the president really said that or not.

So when Thomas and Jacob left the *Sam A. Adams* and stepped ashore in Louisville, they were in the United States, but they were in a state that was not "officially" taking part in the war. And neutral Louisville was serving as an important command city for the Yankee armies. The reason Thomas and Jacob were even in Louisville was to meet with top Union commanders and to pass along Mr. Lincoln's written letters and his oral messages.

Kentucky seemed a mass of contradictions to Jacob. Slavery was legal. In fact, Thomas and Jacob walked past what up until recently had been a very large and prosperous slave auction house, so obviously some Kentuckians supported ideas that the Confederates held dear, like slavery. In fact, in 1861, ignoring their state's official position of neutrality, two full companies of volunteers headed south to fight with the Rebels. Five days later however; three new companies of men were formed. These men headed north to Indiana to enlist in the Union Army.

Abraham Lincoln had been born in Kentucky, but the citizens had not voted for him. He had received less than 1% of their votes. Kentuckians seemed to believe Mr. Lincoln was in league with abolitionists, yet they had also refused to vote for native son John Breckinridge because he was seen as supporting secession. It seemed Kentucky wanted to stay in the Union yet keep their slaves. "I've just had a thought," Jacob said to Thomas as they walked

Louisville's streets, "Kentuckians might have a great deal in common with ex-General McClellan!" Thomas didn't speak but he had given him the hard look.

Though plenty of Kentucky residents might support the Confederacy, Louisville, the state's largest city, had become a stronghold of Union forces. In fact as Thomas and Jacob walked toward their appointment, Louisville held some 80,000 Union soldiers. It held the Brown General Hospital and a camp for Confederate prisoners. It also held the Galt House.

Many people called the Galt House Louisville's best hotel. Why Jefferson Davis, president of the Confederacy, had stayed there. Now, Galt House was used by Union officers as an unofficial headquarters. It was abuzz with Union troops and officers, coming and going all day long. The Galt House was Thomas and Jacob's current destination.

As they made their way up crowded Fourth Street, Jacob suddenly asked, "So what can you tell me about the murder?"

"What murder?"

"You know, General Bull Nelson's murder!" Jacob responded with enthusiasm. "Didn't it happen right there in the main lobby of the Galt House? I mean the very place we're going? Didn't General

Jefferson Davis, (that's his name right?) just shoot
General Nelson in broad daylight? And isn't it true
that General Nelson was his commander? And isn't
true," Jacob pushed on, "that General Nelson was
unarmed? So General Jefferson Davis shot down an
unarmed man, his commanding general in broad
daylight?" Jacob gave Thomas a devilish grin. "And
isn't it true that he got clean away with it?"

Thomas stopped and gazed down at Jacob. "It
seems to me you know all you need to know about
the matter. Please put it away. It's not appropriate for
today's discussion." Thomas turned to resume his
journey to the Galt House.

But he was amazed. Mr. Hay had told Thomas
all about the sordid stunning affair. Jacob's account,
strangely enough, was basically 100% accurate. Now
where had he gotten all that information? Sure
enough, last September General Nelson and General
Davis had had a falling out, and it was as Jacob said.
Nelson and Davis had had an acrimonious encounter
at the Galt House. Davis had obtained a pistol and
shot the unarmed Nelson. Thomas was still amazed
that Davis hadn't been tried and hanged right then,
but the war caused strange things to happen. General
Buell wrote that he did not have enough officers to
spare for a court-martial. With that pronouncement,

Davis had effectively gotten away with murder. *"How does a man flat out get away with murder? And how did Jacob know all that?"* Jacob continued to amaze and surprise him.

Thomas made quick work of his Galt House appointments. After living in Washington City and working at the White House, neither Thomas or Jacob were overly impressed with people just because their jackets held fancy buttons or stars. Rank didn't seem that important when you worked at the White House. What military man outranked the president?

Thomas delivered the president's letters, his messages, his words of encouragement. The Kentucky mission was soon accomplished. With their Kentucky work done, the two turned their eyes northward. It was time to cross that river and visit Indiana.

Chapter 12

"Ready, Jacob? Excited?" Thomas asked. He was busily leaning as far out as he dared over the boat's railing, stretching for the blue-white spray that shot up from the bow.

Strangely, Jacob was nowhere near the spray. He stood with his back pressed firmly placed against the wooden planks of the boat's cabin. His arms were crossed across his chest and his gaze was fixed on the approaching Indiana shoreline. The two companions were ferrying across the Ohio, watching Louisville, Kentucky, shrink away as Jeffersonville, Indiana, grew.

Jacob took a very deep breath. "About as ready as I'm ever going to be," he reluctantly replied.

Thomas turned away from the river and faced Jacob. "Now now, Mister Bunten," he said shaking a finger in Jacob's direction, "no irrational fears."

Jacob didn't think his thoughts were irrational, but he took Thomas' point. Deep down he knew everything was going to be fine. Still to go back to Salem, the place where he had known both so much pain and yes, so much joy, well, he just wasn't sure. He'd lived the majority of his life there with his family and now how strange to be going back as an orphan!

Yes, technically an orphan he thought to himself but lately, he had begun to entertain the strange notion that he might just have stumbled into…well, a family. At least a family of a sort. No blood ties to be sure, but he had come to realize he was in a place where people cared about him and his welfare. In his mind, that made them a kind of a family, a family he had come to care deeply about.

He was most certainly returning to Indiana as a different person. How far he had come! He thought back to the blur of his illness, how close he had come to dying. He knew he was lucky to be alive. He thought about his train trip east, sent to a New York aunt who was cold, unfeeling, unwelcoming, and uncaring. He thought about his escape from that fate, his luck in surviving the First Battle of Bull Run, and the luck of falling in with Mr. Henderson. Thank you, Sergeant Emerson. And then the amazing journey that led to his position at the White House? No, Jacob assured himself, no one would believe his story. Subconsciously, he squared his shoulders and prepared for his return to Indiana.

A few short moments later, the boat docked. Thomas looked around curiously as they departed the ferry. He was very busy taking in his first close look at Indiana, but he didn't say anything.

They had previously agreed to take the advice of the Union officers in Louisville. They'd advised the two to head directly to the Warmont Livery Stable. "Not cheap," warned one captain, "but their mounts are dependable."

"Very serviceable," agreed a major.

Though he had been warned, Thomas still grumbled as they left the stables. "Not cheap?! Expensive as all get out is a better way to put it! Expensive indeed! $125 for a horse," Thomas continued, "and we needed two! Outrageous! Bordering on highway robbery!"

Jacob almost said, "It's not your money!" but he thought better of it. It had been a struggle, but he had learned to occasionally hold his tongue.

Thomas shook his head in aggravation but continued leading the horses away. He had to admit they now owned two fine mounts, and the men at Warmont's had assured him he would be able to sell those fine mounts easily in Indianapolis for every penny he had paid. They even gave him the name of a reputable Indianapolis stable. "Make it a free journey for you, sir," one stablehand had promised. "Hmph!"

Thomas had responded. He was not in the best of moods at the time.

Thomas' mood lightened as they left Jeffersonville and started heading north. Back in Louisville, they had repacked all their belongings. Some were sent on up to Indianapolis via train, some were sent back to the Dodge House in Washington City. Now they rode with their remaining belongings packed into the saddlebags they carried. It was approximately 50 miles to Salem, as the crow flies so they planned on making it a two-day journey.

After some 30 miles they halted in Pekin, Indiana, a stop on the stagecoach run between Louisville and Salem.

They spent a pleasant night at a tavern in Pekin, breakfasted, and resumed their journey. They rode through beautiful rolling hills. Thomas wasn't sure what he thought Indiana would look like, but he did not expect Southern Indiana to be this beautiful or bountiful. The farmers were just preparing fields for planting. War seemed to be far away.

As they rode northwest toward Salem, Thomas offered, "Just like old times, hey Jacob? Just like when we started this adventure."

Jacob took slight issue with his observation. "Well, this time we have two horses instead of one, we didn't get stormed on, we didn't sleep in a barn, and we got breakfast at the tavern instead of eating a farmwife's leftovers out of a cloth rag, but otherwise…"

"Don't be a smart aleck!" Thomas barked. After a minute's pause, he said, "Still I will admit you're right; we have come up a bit in the world."

They rode for a few more minutes. Suddenly, Jacob pointed across a newly plowed field toward a nearby stream, "Shall we water the horses?"

Thomas gave him a confused look. They were not more than ten miles into the journey, but then he realized Jacob had his reasons. Perhaps, Thomas concluded, he wasn't quite ready to arrive in Salem. "But of course," Thomas said. The two rode over the field and led the horses to water. Thomas waited for Jacob to speak. The two horses didn't seem to mind the early break and they took advantage of the cool, clean water.

"Well, uhmm, Mr. Henderson," Jacob started, "I just want to thank you again for all you've done for me." This comment caught Thomas off guard. Was Jacob changing his mind and thinking of staying? But he said nothing and merely nodding his thanks.

"I know this is my old home and all, and I really am looking forward to visiting." Jacob paused, took off his hat and wiped his head. "But I've decided I don't need to speak to anyone." He looked at Thomas as if expecting to receive some push back. He hurried on, "My family's gone and there is really no one I need to see, no one I need to speak to. I'm a different person now. That boy they put on a train for New York doesn't really exist anymore, and they sure won't know the new one." He paused to readjust his hat. Then he put his earlier thoughts into words, "They sure won't understand my new family, and to be honest, they won't even care." He paused for another second and then continued, "And to be really honest, it's none of their business now!" The last few words had an edge to them and he stared straight at Thomas.

A very warm feeling swept over Thomas as he heard Jacob's words. He too believed they had formed a new family in Washington, D.C. He hadn't been sure if Jacob could or would acknowledge it though. Hearing that meant a lot to Thomas.

Thomas took the minute to wipe his head as well. Then he quietly spoke, "Jacob your reasoning seems sound to me. What course of action would you like to follow?"

Jacob smiled and it seemed a weight lifted from his shoulders. "Well, Sir, I'd like to quietly ride through town, picking up memories to share with Mr. Hay."

"Then that's exactly what we'll do." And they did.

They rode past the site of Jacob's father's store and they rode down College Street, of course. They rode right up to Mr. Hay's childhood home. Jacob gave it a long hard look while Thomas took notes. Jacob almost told Thomas the notes weren't necessary but again, he held his tongue.

They rode down Mulberry looking at the house Jacob called the White Mansion. They rode past what used to be his family's farm. They took their time, wandering where they would. They exchanged pleasantries with people, and they stopped in the store to purchase victuals, but Jacob saw no one he recognized.

After a few hours, Thomas reined in and asked, "Any other places to see or visit?"

"No, sir," Jacob said firmly "nothing else here for me now. It was a great visit but that life is over. It's time to head on. "

"Well, sir, if that the case," Thomas said, "let's head north." They pulled their horses back into the road and headed north toward Indianapolis. It was time to finish their mission.

They made their way to one of Indiana's most famous roads, the Michigan Road. That road stretched from Madison northward to Lake Michigan. "From river to lake!" some Hoosiers said. Indianapolis was about halfway between the two. Thomas greatly enjoyed the journey. The landscape changed as they made their way north. Rolling forested hills flattened out to give way to farms which in turn, gave way to the city of Indianapolis.

Thomas was greatly surprised by Indianapolis. Why it was a thriving city! A thriving military city at that. Given its geography, Indianapolis had grown into a major transportation hub. Indianapolis was located right in the middle of the state. Roads and railroads criss-crossed the city. The National Road ran right through the town east to west, the Michigan Road north to south.

Soldiers were everywhere. It appeared Indianapolis had more soldiers than Louisville! Thomas and Jacob saw soldiers of all ranks as they checked into their downtown hotel.

The next day, they made the short walk from the hotel to the state capital for their appointment with Indiana's governor Oliver P. Morton.

After the handshaking and a gracious welcome, Governor Morton ushered them into a very pleasant wood-paneled study. The trio sat down. Thomas pulled the sealed packet from his bag. "Governor Morton, sir, with the president's compliments," he said solemnly. The governor pulled a pair of reading glasses from an inside vest pocket and proceeded to read the president's message, twice. He sighed as he placed the communication down on the table.

"Great man, Abraham Lincoln. The country's blessed to have him. I'll write him a reply, of course, but Mr. Henderson, please let me give you a verbal message to deliver. Please tell the president that I appreciate the help and support and, of course, we will continue to support the war with our utmost!"

"And gentlemen, may I thank you for making the long journey just so you could deliver the message personally. Let me thank you and the president for that gracious gesture. I am humbled, truly."

Thomas felt compelled to jump in. "The president most sincerely wanted to come himself, but the situation in the east compelled him to remain in the Capital. Jacob and I, of course, are poor substitutes but we are pleased to have made the journey."

Governor Morton pushed back quickly, "A poor substitute? Good gracious sir, not at all. Why to have a personal advisor to the president come to our fine state? We're honored, Sir."

Thomas winced at the personal advisor quote, but decided to let that slide by. *"I suppose it is true,"* he wryly thought, *"that I do work at the White House and, on occasion, I have given the president advice. I guess that will have to do."* He chose not to share these thoughts with the governor; he merely smiled his thanks.

The governor insisted on escorting them on a buggy ride around the city. As they rode, he lectured, "We're a Union town, through and through. Did you know President Lincoln stopped right here on his inaugural train trip? Gave a rousing speech. Great man," he said again.

"Do you know" he continued, "that thousands of Hoosiers have volunteered to fight for our cause? Well, I suppose you do know that. But did you know we raised four units right here in the Capital City?" He lifted fingers to count out, "The National Guards, the City Greys, the Indianapolis Independent Zouaves, and the Zouave Guards."

"And did you know we have over 30 military camps, stations, or hospitals right here in Indianapolis?" Again the counting fingers came up,

"Camp Sullivan, Camp Morton, Camp Burnside, Camp Freemont, and Camp Carrington to name just a few!" He took a deep breath but somehow managed to continue talking. "We have a prison for captured Confederates. We have a hospital and an arsenal. We have a large soldiers' home, and our citizens help the war effort day and night!"

With one last large breath, he continued, "And did you know that Richard Jordan Gatling invented and tested his Gatling gun right here in Indianapolis? I believe the U.S. Navy has adopted the Gatling gun and is moving toward putting it in service." The last comment seemed to caused the governor his all and he sank heavily back into this cushioned buggy seat. He seemed to have tuckered himself out for the moment.

Thomas took advantage of the pause and stretched the truth a mite. "Oh, the president told us much of that sir, when he was preparing us for our trip." Thomas gestured out the window as the buggy made it's way around Indianapolis' streets. "It's obvious to see that this is a Union town. It's obvious to see that Indiana supports the war effort." He took a short pause and said, "Perhaps that's why the president sent an Indiana man on this mission."

"What's that?" asked the governor.

"Why, yes, sir, Jacob here is a born and bred Hoosier."

Rarely shy, Jacob jumped right in. "Yes sir. Salem, Indiana. In fact, we've just come from there."

"Is that so?" asked the governor, "and how did a Salem boy come to find himself at the White House?" Thomas settled into his own seat as Jacob began his story. He listened and watched as the two Hoosiers talked.

Upon the ride's completion, the governor kindly invited them to dine. They had a very pleasant meal and then the governor reluctantly prepared to resume his schedule. It was clear he enjoyed and appreciated their visit. He shook both their hands enthusiastically and thanked them profusely for their help. They in turn promised to pass his heartfelt thanks on to the president.

And that ended their Indiana mission. Upon reflection Thomas decided he hadn't really given too much prior thought to Indianapolis or Indiana. He was very pleasantly impressed by both.

The return trip was all rail and all first class. They quickly and easily settled into to life on the rails. They read, caught up on the latest news, and dined well. They also had plenty of time to talk. One afternoon as they finished a fine lunch, Thomas introduced a new topic. "Tell me Jacob, what do you plan to do when the war is won?"

Honestly Jacob had given that subject little thought. What would he do? What did the future hold for an Indiana farm boy come to Washington?

He crunched his face as he answered, "I honestly just do not know, Mr. Henderson. I guess I was waiting to see how the war turned out. Waiting to see what the future might hold." He turned to look out the window before he continued, "Not sure how much a future I might have," he said. "Not sure what the world will be like for someone such as me, an orphaned farm-boy from Indiana."

Thomas resisted the urge to instantly reply. Instead he leaned back, steepled his fingers, and also took a moment to look at the passing scenery. After a few minutes silence, he said, "You know, Jacob, the president said something to me, right before we made this trip." The president's thundering visit to the cranny was still a quite vivid memory for Thomas. "He told me I lacked the eye to see myself as others do." He readjusted his fingers but kept his gaze on the scenery. "He was absolutely right, though it took a bit of time for me to see it." He turned his full attention on Jacob. "I believe you suffer from the same ailment." Before Jacob could protest, he held up his hand asking for a moment.

"I did not agree with the president's assessment at the time, though I was too big a coward to disagree with him to his face." He thought once back to the president's mood that day. No sir, that day he had been quite happy to keep quiet!

"But as the days passed and I gave it more well deserved thought, I realized the president was right. Though I was right as well, in a way. How can anyone see himself as others do? I don't believe you can. However," he said once again holding up the restraining hand, "I believe you can come to understand what others see. And that's what I started working on that day.

So if I may continue my speech, and I know it is a speech, let me share the president's words with you. Well, a paraphrased version of it, fitted to you. Let me ask you, are you not the young man who left Salem, Indiana as an orphan and successfully made your way to Washington, D.C.? Are you not the young man who survived First Bull Run? Are you not the young man who helped me and spent a year studying the Army of the Potomac? Are you not the young man who helped me produce a White House approved analysis of General McClellan? Are you not the young man General Kearny trusted? Did you not make your way during the Peninsula Campaign when I was invalided? Have you not made your way among the highfaluting in Washington, D.C. and most importantly, are you not the young man who has earned the president's trust?"

Thomas' sentences dropped like coins on a collection plate for Jacob. He sat in silence staring at Thomas. His mouth fell slightly open. Luckily, he could not see himself. It was not his best look.

Thomas could not resist, "Uhmm Jacob, with a mouth open like that, I'm told there is a danger of flies…"

Jacob shook his head as if to clear it. "Let me make sure I am understanding you. Are you saying because those things all happened…" Then he paused. After a moment's reckoning, he started again, "Well dad gum it, what are you saying?"

"I guess I'm just saying it's hard to see ourselves as others do. Mr. Lincoln told me he wanted me to make this trip because I was ready to do so. I hadn't seen that, but believe me he was adamant. I'm saying you have earned credit for doing much whether you realize it or not. You may not see it the same way others do, but again believe me when I say people see you as an up and coming young man."

"But I haven't attended school on a regular basis since Indiana!" Jacob protested. "I have no formal training; how can I be up and coming?"

"Well, if I may be forgiven for pointing this out, Mr. Lincoln didn't attend, much less graduate college and look what he's accomplishing! We should all do that much good!"

Jacob had to agree with that. The words sunk in and gave him something to think about as the rail wheels clicked them eastward, eastward toward home.

Chapter 13

"Welcome back intrepid travelers!"

John Hay reached out into the hall, grabbed Thomas with one hand and Jacob with the other, and literally yanked the two into Nicolay's office.

Enthusiastic handshakes and hearty thumps on the backs were exchanged. Nicolay took a minute to step out and call, "Mister President. Our western travelers have returned!" Soon Abraham Lincoln entered the office and joined the fray. He too greeted the pair with a hearty, "Welcome home!"

When they were finally all seated and partially calmed down, Mr. Lincoln reached over and enclosed Jacob's hand with his own two very large hands. He gently shook the hand. He looked the boy straight in the eye as he said with warmth, "Now Jacob, tell me everything about Indiana." Jacob smiled widely and proceeded to do just that.

John Hay leaned in, poised to drink in every memory about Indiana and their shared hometown, Salem, Indiana. Thomas stood ready with his book of notes, but Jacob was true to his word. Jacob recited all his memories without the smallest mistake. He remembered every detail and filled the room with images of Southern Indiana and Salem. Thomas enjoyed watching the three Hoosiers as they talked. The mention of an item, College Street or the White Mansion for instance, would send them into a flurry of reminiscences. For a small bit of time, they were all fully immersed in Salem and Southern Indiana. Thomas was glad for them.

But the men were not satisfied to just hear about Indiana; they wanted to know everything, every last detail about the journey. How was the political temperature in Louisville and Indiana? How were the soldiers? How was Governor Morton? How was the weather? How were the roads? The president even wanted to know all about the *Samuel A. Adams* and their journey down the Ohio. "Made a long river trip once myself, you know," the president told them.

But more than anything, the president wanted to know how the war, and the Emancipation Proclamation were being perceived in the west.

Jacob still aglow from his Indiana narrative answered first, much to the amusement of Misters Hay and Nicolay. "Oh, Mr. Lincoln, you don't have to worry about that!" he assured the smiling president. "We saw thousands of Union men, good Union men, tried and true!" Jacob paused to reconsider. "Maybe hundreds of thousands of them. Way too many to count!"

Thomas spoke up to offer a bit of temperance. "It is most certainly true that we saw a great deal of Union support in both Indiana and Kentucky. And Jacob is right," he said smiling at his companion, "We saw far too many soldiers to count. Of course we were being guided by Union men. Sadly, I'm sure both places have their share of copperheads."

"And as for the Proclamation?" the president asked.

"Ah well, perhaps a bit less fervor there, sir, I have to say."

Jacob jumped back in, "Those folks just don't understand how important it is!" he assured the president.

That made the president laugh again, "Well then, Jacob, it's our job to make sure that they do come to understand it!"

Then the president stood, pulled his pocket watch from his vest, and announced, "Time to return to work." He dropped the watch in his pocket while reaching out to shake hands with Thomas. "Thank you again for going and for all your work. It is most certainly appreciated. I look forward to reading your report."

"And you shall soon have it, sir." Thomas promised.

"I will read it carefully and with great interest," the president promised.

Then there was that small moment of silence that almost always appeared just after President Lincoln exited a room. John Hay broke the spell as he playfully punched Jacob on the shoulder. "So overall, it was a good trip?"

"It's been a great trip!" said Jacob enthusiastically.

"Agreed.' said Thomas. "Very enjoyable, and educational."

And then they both said almost in unison, "But it was a long trip!"

That comment brought a round of laughter from all.

"And it's great to be home." said Jacob.

"Agreed." said Thomas again.

Jacob said, "Oh, but it's really good to be home again."

Returning to the moment, Thomas asked, "So what's the news here? You've heard all we know. What have we missed?"

"Oh, we have a new addition to the family," said an obviously pleased John Hay. "We have a new state in the Union!" He'd had a hand in helping the president with this issue and he was obviously proud of his efforts. "Yes, sir," he continued, "West Virginia is our newest addition. The president signed the paperwork just the other day, and we're looking to add Nevada soon as well! "

"New states!" said Jacob with amazement. "That's big news."

"Indeed!" said John Hay, puffing up a bit.

"Indeed," said Nicolay a bit dryly. "And of course, the other obvious news is that you've brought spring home with you." said Nicolay. He gave Thomas a knowing look, "And you know what that means."

"Armies on the move." Thomas replied, nodding his head to Nicolay.

"Armies are on the move." Hay agreed.

"And our new commanding general?" Thomas asked cautiously.

John Hay wandered over to the window and gazed out for a minute before answering. "Well that question is a little bit hard to answer."

"What's wrong?" Thomas asked in alarm.

Hay tamped his hands down to comfort the younger man, "No, no, nothing's exactly wrong, it's just…"

Nicolay continued the thought, "Well, our new commander is being quite loquacious."

That brought Jacob into the conversation. "Loquacious?" he asked.

Thomas nodded at him. "It seems our new commander has a lot to say," he explained.

"Well," Jacob responded "that was going on before we left. Remember all that about the country needing a dictator?" Jacob wrinkled his nose. "Never did like all that talk."

"And don't forget," John Hay added "that bit about 'may God have mercy on Bobby Lee, for I shall have none.'"

This time Nicolay waved his hands around as if to dismiss Hay's statement and clear the air. "Now to be fair, the morale in the army has greatly improved, and he appears to have a strong plan in place."

"Ah, but," John Hay interjected, "he's yet to meet Lee in battle." He paused again. looking at the others "and I'm worried."

It turned out he had good reason to be.

On April 4, Lincoln left the capital to spend a few days with his new commander. He met General Hooker near Fredericksburg, Virginia. During their meetings Lincoln reminded Hooker that his "primary object is the enemies army in front of you, and is not with or about Richmond." Hooker assured the president that he fully understood.

When the president left, Hooker went to work refining his battle plan. On paper, it looked very promising. He would send General George Stoneman and his 10,000 cavalrymen across the Rappahannock River. Their job would be to raid the Confederate rear, cutting Lee's communication lines and destroying supplies. Hooker believed this action would force Lee to abandon his fortified positions on the Rappahannock and withdraw toward his capital. Hooker could attack as Lee retreated.

But Hooker learned how true the folk saying was, "Man plans, nature laughs." Stonemen attempted to cross, but heavy rains made crossing rivers or even streams impossible. Learning of this, President Lincoln told Nicolay, "I greatly fear it is another failure already." Hooker was forced back to the drawing board.

But back at that drawing board he was determined to create a plan that would destroy Lee and his army. His second plan called for the Army of the Potomac to attempt an audacious double envelopment of Lee's entire army. Hooker believed this move would force one of two actions. Either Lee would be forced to retreat, in which case Hooker would quickly pursue, or Lee would be forced to attack the Union Army on terrain of Hooker's choosing. Hooker saw it as a win-win proposition.

On April 19, Hooker shared his plan with President Lincoln, Secretary of War Edwin M. Stanton, and General-in-Chief Henry W. Halleck. Then he made a proclamation for his army, "The operations of the last three days have determined that our enemy must ingloriously fly or come out from behind their defences and give us battle on our ground, where certain destruction awaits him."

Hooker was so confident that he then told a reporter, "The Rebel army is the legitimate property of the Army of the Potomac. They may as well pack up their haversacks and make for Richmond." The reporter wrote it down, but he shook his head as he did so. He had heard such proclamations before. He had covered McClellan.

On April 27, the Army of the Potomac started moving. They were able to cross both the Rappahannock and Rapidan Rivers. So far, so good. By April 30, the army was concentrating about 12 miles west of Fredericksburg. They happened to gather around a large brick mansion located on the Orange Turnpike. The home was owned by the

Chancellor family. The area was called Chancellorsville. General Hooker's plan was in action. Things looked promising for the North.

But he was not the only general with a plan. Robert E. Lee had been watching the approaching Army of the Potomac closely. His intelligence gathering told him he was outnumbered nearly two to one. He realized Hooker had troops near Fredericksburg and Chancellorsville. But which force was the real attacking force? What was Hooker's main intention? Was he truly splitting his army or was one of the two a feint?

One section of the Union army advanced from Chancellorsville into an overgrown area known locally as the Wilderness. Though this area was covered with thick undergrowth, the men made progress. By the evening of April 30, they had advanced closer to Lee's flank.

Some generals would have seen this approach, seen the size of the opposing army and decided that a quick retreat was the best option. Not Robert E. Lee. On May 1, the two armies' front lines clashed. Word was quickly sent back to General Hooker that the enemy had been engaged. Hooker to almost everyone's amazement, ordered the army to retreat back to Chancellorsville.

Many of his commanders immediately objected. Give up the ground they'd already won? Surely not! They'd fought their way out of the Wilderness for the most part, and some, like General George Meade's troops, actually occupied the high ground. They stood to move on Lee's flank. Retreat? Insanity! General Meade was so unhappy he declared, "My God if we can't hold the top of the hill, we certainly can't hold the bottom of it!"

They decided Hooker must not truly understand the gains they had made. They wrote Hooker that they had taken the high ground and had cleared the Wilderness. They were in an excellent position they assured their commanding general.

Hooker's second in command, General Darius N. Couch decided that a letter would not do. He needed to ride back and speak with Hooker in person. He later wrote that before this meeting Hooker had been *all vigor, energy and activity.* The Hooker that he now met however seemed depressed, listless and trancelike. When Couch made his plea, Hooker responded, "It's all right, Couch, I've got Lee just where I want him." Couch left. "I retired from his presence with the belief that my commanding general was a whipped man." That evening, Hooker sent a message to his corps commanders, "The major general

commanding trusts that a suspension in the attack today will embolden the enemy to attack him."

The Union generals were not the only ones
surprised by Hooker's actions. Lee summoned his
commanders and ordered an evening conference to
discuss the situation. General Robert E. Lee and
General Thomas "Stonewall" Jackson met at the
intersection of the Plank Road and the Furnace Road
to plan their next move.

Jackson offered the opinion that Hooker might
use the next day to retreat across the Rappahannock
but Lee disagreed. He believed Hooker planned to
stay, hoping Lee's smaller army would attack his
larger, entrenched army. As they sat together on that
evening of May 1, Hooker had approximately 130,000
men; Lee commanded around 60,000. That certainly
appeared to be disturbing news for the South.

But as they sat by the fire that evening, more
and more information filtered in. Eventually General
J.E.B. Stuart brought the news that while both the
front and left flanks were entrenched, the right flank
was *"in the air"*. This meant it was susceptible to
attack. A flank susceptible to attack was welcome
news. However the welcome was dampened a bit by
the realization that the *"in the air"* flank was some ten
to twelve miles west of their current position. That

meant troops would be on the march for several hours.

As Lee and Jackson continued to talk, a few things became clear. The attack could work, but only if Jackson could make the long march undetected and only if Hooker's army stayed right where it was. Perhaps most importantly, it also meant that Lee must successfully divide his army. He would be sending men on a march that took them completely out of the conflict for several hours.

Then Jackson's cartographer, Jedediah Hotchkiss, brought news of a road that would allow the troops to make that twelve-mile march hidden from Union eyes. When Lee asked Jackson how many men he would take on the flanking march, Jackson replied, "My whole command." That meant some 28,000 to 30,000 men would be marching away from the rest of Lee's army. It also meant that if Hooker attacked Lee's smaller force, they could well be destroyed. Every military textbook in the world said that this was a bad idea. Lee remembered the textbook's advice, considered all the factors facing him and then directed Jackson to make the flanking march.

So on the morning of May 2, General Thomas "Stonewall" Jackson sent his men on a long march around the Union Army. General J.E.B. Stuart's cavalry tried to shield the marching Confederates. They did their best, but the marching men were seen. The Army of the Potomac had a balloon, the *Eagle,* that was used for reconnaissance. That day it flew right over the marching Confederates. The Rebels were sure they were caught out, but evidently the soldiers in the *Eagle* thought the men were of little import. The *Eagle* sent no report about marching Confederates to Union headquarters.

Other Union soldiers caught glimpses of the Rebels. One officer reported that he'd been watching Confederates march by for almost three hours. When these reports reached Hooker, he made two responses. One was to send General Howard, who commanded the right flank, a warning that he might be in danger of being attacked and that he should prepare. The other was to tell officers that if the Rebels were truly marching, he was sure it meant they were retreating.

General Howard took no defensive action; Hooker did nothing else to address the move and later that afternoon, Stonewall Jackson's men burst out of the Wilderness directly onto Howard's XI Corp.

As the Rebels approached, many Union troops were just starting to assemble evening meals. Sitting, talking, brewing coffee, or preparing meals, they were amazed to look up and see animals running from the forest toward them. Now why in the world would animals be leaving the safety of the forest to run toward men? The men did not quite yet know that the animals were fleeing the oncoming Rebel wave. They soon found that out. They found out the animals were running for their lives. Soon the Union troops were running for theirs. Jackson's men came storming out of that forest, screaming the Rebel Yell and storming directly upon them.

Later, observers would call Chancellorsville *"Lee's greatest battle"* because of his audacious decision to divide his army in front of a much larger force. It was a stunning victory. The Army of the Potomac was defeated again. A smaller force had crushed the larger enemy, and Union soldiers were retreating toward Washington, D. C. once again.

The cost of the battle was high for both sides. The North suffered over 17,000 casualties. The South suffered over 12,000. One of the South's casualties was Stonewall Jackson.

Jackson's march had taken longer than he wanted and his men did not get into action until nearly 5:00 p.m. Their success was immediate and impressive, but Jackson wanted more. As the twilight gave way to evening, Jackson rode out in front of his lines, searching for a way to inflict more casualties on the Army of the Potomac. When one of his staff officers warned him about the dangerous position, Jackson replied, "The danger is all over. The enemy is routed." They rode on.

Confederate soldiers from North Carolina on the lookout for Union soldiers saw the riders. They opened fire believing they were shooting Union troops. Instead they were wounding their commanding officer. A few days later, Jackson died as a result of those wounds.

Meanwhile, Hooker was retreating, but he was not yet safe. Lee was pressing him, and he also had to fight Mother Nature. Rains once again made it extremely difficult to cross Virginia's rivers and streams. Hooker almost lost his pontoon bridges, his key to getting north. But the army managed to get across the angry river, and the men were glad to cut those bridges free. They were glad to let the current take those bridges where it would. Safely across, some of the soldiers found it ironic that they had crossed at a point called U.S. Ford.

In Washington, the newspaperman Noah Brooks, a friend of the president, happened to be there when the president read the report of the fiasco.

Brooks wrote of Lincoln, "The sight of his face and figure was frightful, he seemed stricken with death. Almost tottering to a chair, he sat down. His face was of the same color as the wall behind him—not pale, not even sallow, but gray, like ashes." President Abraham Lincoln looked up and moaned, "My God! My God! What will the country say?" Seeing the president, Secretary of War Stanton did not want the president left alone. He feared that President Lincoln might commit suicide.

But as he always had done before, Mr. Lincoln pulled himself together. He knew if he gave in to the endless grief that tormented his soul, the country he loved would be destroyed. Like those in the field, Mr. Lincoln put his head down. He returned to the task at hand. He returned to work.

So did Thomas and Jacob. Jacob was almost beside himself with the defeat. "But we went west!" as if that trip had somehow made a difference to this battle. "And what about all those things Hooker said? What happened with all that? And what about that stuff about the Rebel army being our property? What about packing up their haversacks and making for Richmond?"

No one could answer those questions. And there were lots of other questions as well. As Thomas studied, sorted, and delivered the reports, he kept coming back to two specific questions. First, why had the North lost? They had outnumbered the enemy at least two to on; Hooker had created a realistic plan. In the beginning the plan had worked. The army, specifically Meade's men, had made good progress. But then what? Why had Hooker ordered that retreat? How had he let Stonewall and Lee make such a stunning move?

"Now to be fair, Thomas," Nicolay said. "It is true that General Hooker was almost killed by cannon fire. That has to affect a man greatly."

"True," said John Hay, drawing out the word. "The cannonball hit the very porch pillar he was leaning against. I heard it threw him around like a rag doll."

Hooker later wrote that half of the pillar "violently struck me ... in an erect position from my head to my feet."

"And I hear he was clearly dazed," Nicolay added.

"That so?" Jacob shrewdly asked, "Then why didn't he give up command to his second, General Couch? The way I hear, Couch was right there, ready to serve. If Hooker's so all shook up, he shouldn't be making decisions anyway, right?"

"Perhaps," Thomas the peacemaker said, "he didn't realize he was not making sense."

"Humph!" Jacob snorted, "not sure about that!"

"To be fair, again, Jacob, General Hooker did turn command of the army over to General Couch," Nicolay said, examining a report to confirm his accuracy.

"But John, was it not later in the day and before he relinquished command, did he also not order General Couch to retreat? Correct?" And then Hay pushed on, "And let's not forget," Hay said, "this cannonball incident came the day after he had ordered the first retreat, you know the retreat of Meade's men and all. Now how does that excuse him?"

Thomas had no answer for Jacob's questions; he had no answers for John's. He did have a theory. As he studied everything, it seemed to him that Hooker, like Burnside, may have been given a job that was simply too big for him. He'd lost confidence in himself, it seemed to Thomas. Hooker had lost confidence in Hooker, and the head injury certainly did not help,

The second question that was perplexing Thomas might be the more important of the two. It was clear Hooker was not the man to lead Mr. Lincoln's armies. So they were back to that seeming age-old question again, if not Hooker, who? Who could successfully lead this army?

Clearly, it was not an easy question because it was not an easy task. Thomas had learned so much since he came stumbling out of William and Mary as he put it. To the uninformed, generalling might look easy. You look at a piece of paper, a map, and you say "Do this, move this way with that, go that way with that, win the battle. If you lose, you look at your opposition. Do what they do. There, job done." But Thomas knew that was all so much nonsense. It was not that easy. His time on the peninsula had certainly shown him that. It was a huge struggle, a huge undertaking. There were so many ever changing conditions or unknowns that had to be taken into account; geography, weather, orders obeyed, orders ignored. It never seemed to be as easy as moving pieces on a chessboard.

Some men seemed to be able to master parts of the job McClellan in training for instance, perhaps Burnsides and Hooker in planning. But pulling it all together and executing, well Thomas had yet to see the man who could do that. *"There must be one man who could do it all, isn't there?"* Thomas was no longer sure.

Mr. Lincoln of course was asking the same question. "And frankly," the president had to admit, "I don't know the answer." Mr. Lincoln had walked to the War Department, once again searching for answers. He asked the ever-present lieutenants to lay out a map of the United States. As he gazed down at the map, he found nothing but trouble.

His hand reached toward Mississippi. Grant was still firmly mired in the Mississippi mud. He looked at Virginia. The Army of the Potomac was defeated and retreating northward again. Lee looked free to make whatever move he wanted.

Mr. Lincoln looked at the calendar hanging on the wall. He also looked at the clock. Both were moving much too quickly for him. He murmured, "Time is running out."

Mr. Lincoln very much wanted to win this war. He believed in his oath to protect the Constitution. He believed that preserving the Union was his most important job, the action the Founding Fathers would have wanted.

In his second Inaugural address, given just a few months before, he had written, "In giving freedom to the slave we assure freedom to the free —

honorable alike in what we give and what we preserve. We shall nobly save or meanly lose the last best hope of earth." The last best hope on earth. Mr. Lincoln firmly believed that the United States was exactly that, the last best hope. And that hope must be preserved.

And he believed it not only must be preserved, but that the country must move forward. The United States could not return to the time when enslaving people was legal and even considered moral by some. That horrendous practice must end, and as he wrote in the Emancipation Proclamation, it would. Well, it would if he had his way.

But would he have his way? To accomplish what he so fervently desired, Mr. Lincoln was sure he would have to be reelected. The country would have to chance to select a president again in some 18-months time. He fully intended to run. Would the country have him?

As he glanced again at the calendar, he worried. According to his personal calculations, the odds of reelection looked slim. The people were tired of war; they were tired of defeats; they were tired of casualties. Mr. Lincoln could not blame them, but he could also not stop trying to preserve the Union. He had sworn that oath, that oath to uphold the

Constitution. He firmly intended to do that. "But, right now," he admitted to himself, " I don't see a way to accomplish my goal." Once again, the weight on his shoulders seemed oppressive.

He gave himself a shake and straightened up. He allowed himself one small minute. Then he bid the clerks goodnight and started his return to the White House. As he walked, he couldn't help asking himself, *"Are the wheels falling off the wagon? Have the wheels fallen off the wagon?"*

Sighing, Mr. Lincoln walked into the twilight. As he walked, the twilight gave way to darkness.

Chapter 14

"Mr. Lincoln! Mr. Lincoln! The best of news! Yes sir, the best of news! The type of news that is hard to believe!" John Hay could barely contain himself as he pushed into the president's office. He didn't even stop to give a perfunctory knock on the doorframe.

"As suddenly as that, Grant is out of the Mississippi mud! Dana just sent word," Hay waved a piece of paper above his head, "His telegram just came in! Grant is on the move. Not only the move, but he's finding success. Huzzah! Spring has evidently brought new life to the Union army and the Brown Water Navy. Huzzah!"

President Lincoln and John Nicolay had been seated at a table in the president's office. Now Lincoln partially rose and almost grabbed the telegram from John Hay's hand. He sat back down heavily and began reading. He stopped almost instantly as the exasperation and frustration that had been bedeviling him boiled over. "Hard Times, Louisiana? Bruinsburg, Mississippi? Why don't these telegrams say Vicksburg, Mississippi? Mr. Hay, I need a map!"

As John Hay scurried to find a map, Mr. Lincoln settled his reading glasses on the bridge of his nose, scowled, leaned over, and began reading the telegrams. As he read, a metamorphosis occurred. His shoulders began to unclench. His posture gradually improved. His breathing actually slowed. By the time he had finished his first read of the news, he was smiling. His exasperation and frustration seemed to have evaporated in the May breeze.

Mr. Hay and Mr. Nicolay were stunned by the change and waited as patiently as they could for the news.

Finishing his second reading, Mr. Lincoln smiled broadly at his secretaries. "Well gentlemen, it is not over by any means, but it is well started. Let me give you the summary according to Mr. Dana. Here is what I know so far."

"After spending four months trying to dig canals, move through marshes, redirect the Mississippi River..."

Before he could even think about what he was saying, John Hay interrupted, "And what in the world was that about anyway?"

Mr. Lincoln caused him to blush with a single look. "Hu-hmphh, as I was saying, Mr. Dana quotes Grant as saying most of that was just to keep the army busy. When spring came; however, Grant put his real plan into motion. Gentlemen, earlier this month General Grant marched his army south. Not all his men," Mr. Lincoln quickly amended. "He left Sherman camped right where he was; lighting fires, making noise, doing everything he could to convince the Rebs that the army was just where they thought it was. He even had Sherman demonstrate against the Rebels to convince them everything was as it had been.

At basically the same time, he sent General Grierson and his cavalry on a raid far east of Vicksburg. Grierson had great success riding through the state, pulling Rebels after him and destroying what he could. All the Rebels focused their attention on Sherman and Grierson. Grant said Grierson's raid "knocked the heart out of the state." While Grierson and Sherman were playing their roles, Grant marched the bulk of his army southward on the Louisiana side of the Mississippi River."

Mr. Lincoln consulted the telegram again before continuing. "Dana says they'd hope to cross at Hard Times, Louisiana, moving into Grand Gulf, Mississippi. But that move was thwarted when it turned out the Rebs had fortified Grand Gulf. So rather than plunge into a head-long attack, Grant selected another landing point, Rodney, Mississippi, some thirty miles south."

He returned to the telegram once again. Then he looked up at his listeners with a surprised look on his face. "Well, I'll be. A slave approached Union forces with the news that there was a closer undefended crossing, a place called Bruinsburg, Mississippi. That's why we're reading those two names!" Mr. Lincoln happily concluded.

Impatiently John Hay asked, "So they did indeed make the crossing there?"

Mr. Lincoln laughed, "Yes, my impatient young friend, Dana reports 17,000 Union troops crossed. We are in Mississippi and below Vicksburg!" Mr. Lincoln paused to consider the impact of his words. "And that is great news indeed."

Mr. Lincoln returned to his reading. "Dana concludes that there were a series of engagements, all won by us. Port Gibson, Raymond..." and there the president stopped his reporting. Suddenly, Mr. Lincoln surprised both men by guffawing. He nearly bent over with the laughter. Regaining his composure slightly, he rubbed his eyes, and then turned to his secretaries. "Oh, gentlemen, Mr. Dana must have included this snippet just for me. I simply have to share this story. It's too good not to. Evidently, as the battle of Raymond began to unfold, the town's women, sure their soldiers would carry the day, decided to greet the returning victors and reward them with a picnic." Mr. Lincoln paused to look at his audience.

"So," he continued, "the ladies went to work in their kitchens and ovens preparing a feast of hams, turkeys, cakes, pies, and the like. They spread it all on tables around the courthouse, waiting for their triumphant soldiers to return. Well sure enough the Rebels did return to Raymond but they were running too fast to eat. Hot on their heels came our victorious forces. The Rebels ran right past the tables, but our boys, smart enough not to miss a free meal, settled right in and enjoyed the vittles. Thus ended the Battle of Raymond!" He laughed and rubbed his eyes again. Then he gently placed the telegrams on the table.

"And that concludes the good Mr. Dana's report. Well almost, he does end by saying Grant sent a much more complete report to General Halleck by messenger." Lincoln paused to do the mental calculations. "And that report should be getting here any day now. John, please send a note to General Halleck alerting him to the fact that I want to see that report the moment," he paused and shook his finger at John Hay, "the very moment it arrives."

John Hay merely nodded and said "It shall be done, Mr. Lincoln," as he exited the room.

Mr. Lincoln"s calculations were accurate and two days later, he had Grant's full report of the situation. The report brought many details but actually provided little new information. It did prove however that Mr. Dana was sending very accurate reports to the president.

"Mr. Nicolay, would you please telegraph Mr. Dana and instruct him to send us as much new information as he can? I don't care if it ties up the lines for a week and uses all the paper script in the country. I want information! I want to know what is happening in Mississippi!"

It turned out a lot was happening in Mississippi. After crossing the Mississippi and landing troops in Bruinsburg, Grant considering pushing directly north toward Vicksburg. But as he studied, he realized he would be caught between two rivers, the Mississippi and the Big Black. He saw few usable roads. He also realized the terrain was a series of ridges and valleys, terrain that could prove to be a very costly trap.

So once again instead of just plunging ahead, Grant changed his plans. He ordered his forces to swing east and north. Instead of attacking Vicksburg, Grant decided to cut the enemy's supply and communication line by destroying sections of the railroad that ran west to east, Vicksburg to Jackson. Then to make sure he was not attacked from an eastern force, he turned his attention to the east, to Jackson, Mississippi, the state's capital. Once he captured that city, he was ready to turn his full attention on Vicksburg.

The Rebels realized what Grant was attempting, but they could not stop him. Dana wired that the Confederate defender of Vicksburg, General Pemberton, left the defenses of Vicksburg to challenge Grant. However, Grant's forces were too much for the Confederates. Soon, the Confederates were forced back to Vicksburg.

The Confederates returned safely to the city, but once there, they soon realized they had returned to a desperate situation. No help was coming for them in the way of reinforcements, and the Yankee army came up to completely surround the city. The Rebels were trapped. General Grant settled in and decided to lay siege to the city.

Things began looking bleak for the Confederates almost immediately. The city could not receive any more food or rations. What had been a full day's meal became two day's. Then three. Then four.

The North constantly bombarded the city. Some residents left their exposed houses and sought shelter in caves near the town. Some people went so far as to place carpet on the floor and pictures on the walls of their new dug out homes.

Pemberton could do nothing. He could not get supplies; no army was coming to his rescue. After six weeks of siege, the Confederate commander received a note, "If you can't feed us, you had better surrender us, horrible as the idea is." It was signed 'many soldiers'.

Ironically Pemberton was a Northerner. He was from Pennsylvania. He fought for the Confederacy because he had married a Virginian. When it was time to discuss surrender, Pemberton assured his subordinates, "Make it the Fourth of July, I know my people, they will be more generous then." Grant had won. The North had Vicksburg.

Five days later Port Hudson fell and the North had full control of the Mississippi River. As President Lincoln said, "The father of waters once again goes unvexed to the sea." One week later an unarmed ship sailed from St. Louis down to New Orleans.

All over the country, Grant was recognized as the undisputed victor of the Vicksburg Campaign. He was rewarded for his victory with a promotion to major general in the regular army effective on July 4, 1863. He also received an unusual letter:

"My dear General

I do not remember that you and I ever met personally. I write this now as a grateful acknowledgment for the almost inestimable service you have done the country. I wish to say a word further. When you first reached the vicinity of Vicksburg, I thought you should do, what you finally did—march the troops across the neck, run the batteries with the transports, and thus go below; and I never had any faith, except a general hope that you knew better than I, that the Yazoo Pass expedition, and the like, could succeed. When you got below, and took Port Gibson, Grand Gulf, and vicinity, I thought you should go down the river and join Gen. Banks; and when you turned Northward East of the Big Black, I feared it was a mistake. I now wish to make the personal acknowledgment that you were right, and I was wrong.

Yours very truly,
A. Lincoln"

Thomas made a bit of a deal about sharing Mr. Lincoln's note with Jacob. "Now that is the mark of a great man!" he assured Jacob.

Jacob smiled happily and said, "And best of all, it's settled now!"

Thomas gave him a puzzled look. "All settled? What's all settled? Vicksburg?"

"No sir," came the prompt reply. "Well yes sir. Vicksburg is settled as is leadership of the army. Mr. Lincoln has found himself a general!"

And that did seem to be the obvious answer. Hooker clearly was not working out; Grant had the west well in hand. Why not bring him east and put him in command?

Turns out there were two answers to that question. One - President Lincoln was not sure he wanted Grant to come east and take command and two - Grant wasn't sure he wanted to come east and take command.

Perhaps the matter wasn't settled after all.

Mr. Lincoln Needs A General

Michal Howden

www.michalhowden.com

Made in the USA
Middletown, DE
31 May 2023

31810410R00128